Pina Coladas and Rats

By: Angel Ramon

Copyright © 2023 by Angel Ramon
All Rights Reserved

Book Design by José Manuel Bethencourt Suárez
No part of this book may be reproduced in any form or by any electronic or mechanical means including information storage and retrieval systems, without permission in writing from the author. The only exception is by a reviewer, who may quote short excerpts in a review.
This book is a work of fiction. Names, characters, places, and incidents either are products of the author's imagination or are used fictitiously. Any resemblance to actual persons, living or dead, events, or locales is entirely coincidental.
Angel Ramon

Table of Contents

Note from the Author	5
Chapter 1	6
Chapter 2	14
Chapter 3	20
Chapter 4	25
Chapter 5	33
Chapter 6	42
Chapter 7	51
Chapter 8	60
Chapter 9	67
Chapter 10	77
Chapter 11	84
Chapter 12	96
Chapter 13	104
Chapter 14	113
Chapter 15	120
Chapter 16	127
Chapter 17	134
Chapter 18	141
Chapter 19	147
Chapter 20	155
Chapter 21	161
Chapter 22	167

Chapter 23 _____ 175
Chapter 24 _____ 181
Some cool sites to check out!_____ 189

Note from the Author

Thanks for reading, Pina Coladas and Rats. It takes me a lot of time to write these books. So your investment in time is well appreciated. I just wanted to take the time to thank some important people. First, I want to thank Jack Childress for continuing to believe in me and introducing me to the next person I'll mention.

Special thanks goes to Derek Barton. He was the one who got me to write this story. He intended on starting a horror magazine called, With Malice Magazine. Sadly, it went belly up. The intention was to have story told in parts between issues. When that wasn't an option, I decided to expand upon the story and release it to you legends. In fact, I already have plans of a sequel if enough people read the story. Derek, thank you for believing in my story and getting me to write it.

Finally, thank you to all my fans who believe in me. You are the real all-stars. Without you, I would be talking to myself still.

I must admit, this story is what brought the joy of writing back to me. This was a lot of fun to write. I always had a soft spot for horror. I hope you all enjoy. Please leave a review, it's important to us indie authors.

Chapter 1

Salinas, Puerto Rico – April 9th, 1985

It was an uncharacteristically rainy day in Salinas, Puerto Rico. It was the middle of April. It was normally the dry season on the island. However, on this fateful day, it was anything but sunny. The skies were an eerie dark gray. Thunder was heard while the rain fell heavily. This was the dawn of what would be a dark day for the quaint town.

In a farm, a small pack of rats were crawling. They looked innocent enough as they fed off wheat grains that were growing. The rain didn't seem to bother them. A farmer came out of his house and spotted the rats. He scared them out of the wheat field. The rats ran from the farmer, looking for a place to hide.

***

In a quiet neighborhood back in New York City was a humble woman named Otilia. She was a woman in her upper 30s born in El Salvador. Due to the civil war there, she moved to the United States. There she married her husband, Ruben.

Life in New York was becoming stressful. The couple had saved enough money to buy a beautiful house in Puerto Rico. While Otilia wasn't from the island, Ruben was. He was born on the island, but his parents moved to New York when he was only two. He and Otilia were in search of a tranquil life. New York had become too rowdy as crime increased at an alarming rate.

The two of them bought their dream home in an upstart neighborhood built on an existing sugar plantation. It was relatively cheap, coming in at a price tag of only thirty-five thousand dollars.

On April 9th, 1985, Otilia and her husband took a one-way flight to Puerto Rico. They would leave everything they had in New York, including family, to pursue their love nest.

April 10th, 1985

When they reached the airport in San Juan, the two of them were in awe of the beautiful weather. The sun was warm but not overly hot. There was a nice breeze coming from the Atlantic Ocean.

"I think we're going to love it out here," Ruben told his wife.

"It's like being back in my home country," Otilia replied.

The palm trees were the highlight of the airport. Ruben had the address to the house. While he and his wife took the trip to Puerto Rico, they left a good friend of theirs the keys to their home. His name was Frank.

Frank was in charge of guiding the movers to bring everything into the house. He was only responsible for ensuring everything arrived all in one piece. Later, he would help out Ruben and Otilia fix up the house. Frank also ensured none of the movers got any ideas of stealing jewelry or anything of that nature.

Ruben's car would be shipped by boat to San Juan on a later day. Frank would drive him to the port to pick it up. The new house had its utilities turned on. Frank heard the phone ring as the movers brought the stuff into the house. He had installed a temporary rotary phone into the phone jack to keep in contact with Ruben. Otilia and Ruben had activated the utilities beforehand.

When Frank picked up the phone, he heard Ruben on the phone.

"What happened? Have you arrived in Puerto Rico?" Frank asked in Spanish.

"Yes, I'm at the airport. I'm about to get a taxi to drive me there. Everything ok, there?" Ruben asked.

"The movers are here bringing in your stuff. They should be done by the time you get here."

"Very good! I'm too excited."

"Yo se! Bienvendo a Puerto Rico, que disfrute!" Frank welcomed Ruben to Puerto Rico.

"Gracias." Ruben and Otilia thanked Frank.

Frank hung up the phone. As he put the phone down, he felt a bit guilty. That was because the homes were constructed over sugar plantations. He remembered that his father worked on the plantations. Salinas was one of the last neighborhoods to begin modernizing itself.

While most of Puerto Rico had malls and modern phone lines, Salinas was still stuck in the 60s and 70s. Phone workers were replacing the phone line with modern wiring.

However, the bigger problem was that the construction uncovered a concerning issue in this quaint neighborhood. There was an increase in the mice and rat populations. Mice thrived in the warm weather and Salinas was no exception to mice infestations.

The sugar plantations did a good job controlling the mice population. Or at least one would think. However, since Salinas was a fledging town, it was barely noticeable. The population of Salinas was barely above twenty-thousand people. That number was rather misleading as Salinas was one of the largest towns in Puerto Rico when it came to land size.

Much of the town was still rural with a few bustling villages. The most populated portion was the town center. With the population spread so thin, the mice population was barely noticeable. Many mice ended up on farms. The rodents rarely broke into homes habited by residents.

Things were changing, though. Development in Salinas was accelerating. That meant there was more opportunity for residents to bump into these rodents. After all, mice loved homes since they could multiply and start large families. The population in Salinas was less than twenty thousand at the start of the 80s but had exploded well into the decade.

Frank felt terrible that he didn't tell Ruben and Otilia about the increasing rat population. He figured that they had dealt with rodents in New York City.

"I'm probably worried about nothing. They might even laugh at me for being scared of a stupid mouse," he laughed at himself.

When he looked behind him, Frank saw a mouse running around the house. He chased it out of the house. The mouse was too fast to be caught. Frank didn't see mice as much of a menace.

"Ah, it's not like a mouse can kill," Frank told himself.

He walked to the backyard to get a breeze. The sun was still not out. At least it was only drizzling instead of the heavy downpours from the previous day. Nonetheless, Frank hoped it would clear up. He wanted to hang out by the beach when his friends got to the house. The clouds hung tough with no sign of breaking up.

"Oh well, as long as it doesn't rain like crazy, it should be ok," he said to himself.

Before heading back to the house, Frank heard a loud screech that spooked him. He looked around the yard carefully to see what the noise was. Armed with a bat, Franked looked around in case it was a rat. While mice weren't scary, rats were.

He scoured the entire yard only to come up empty. Frank was relieved to see it was only a product of his imagination. As he walked into the house, Frank heard the screech again. This time, though, he concluded it was one of the workers playing around.

"Get to work, pendejo!" Frank told one of the workers angrily.

Later that day, the workers finished bringing the stuff in. Frank gave the four workers a tip and sent them on their way. While the distance from San Juan to Salinas wasn't too long, the highway was being improved. So he figured that Ruben and Otilia would be delayed.

Within thirty minutes of the movers finishing, Frank saw a taxi arrive. He was excited to see his friends arriving from New York. Before greeting them, he heard the loud screech again. The workers were long gone, so he wasn't sure what was making that noise.

He didn't want to scare off his friends, so he brushed it off. Frank walked to the taxi to help Ruben and Otilia with their luggage. Frank and his friends hugged each other.

"I'm so happy you're finally here. We're going to be neighbors!" Frank was over the moon.

"Where's the sun?" Otilia asked.

"It was sunny in San Juan," Ruben said.

"It's been raining here since Tuesday. However, I'm sure it'll clear up. After all, it's the dry season," Frank tried to reassure the couple.

However, he lied. It was raining in Salinas for four consecutive days, not two. He didn't want to scare his friends, though. Once Ruben and Otilia finished getting their stuff into the house, they knew they had lots of work to do to fully move in. Ruben was thrilled with the idea of having a child in a safer neighborhood. For now, they were all ready to relax.

Frank told them to get ready as he wanted to go to the beach. The sun had peeked while they were unpacking. When they got outside, the sun had disappeared again.

"Oh dear, there goes our day out," Ruben said.

"I swore the weatherman said it wasn't going to rain anymore," Frank replied.

"It's probably only a passing shower," Otilia reassured the men.

The rain came down in earnest and didn't let up for the rest of the day. Temperatures were very cool, not getting out of the 70s for highs. It wasn't exactly the welcome Ruben and Otilia welcomed. They called the local restaurant to order take-out food since the stove wasn't installed yet.

As everyone waited, Otilia looked to her right and saw a mouse. She panicked and ran to the other side of the living room. Ruben grabbed a broom and smacked the mouse, killing it.

"What are you so scared of? It's only a baby mouse. We've seen them in NYC so many times," Ruben asked his wife.

"Eww... why is its blood green?" Otilia asked in horror.

"I'm not sure, but it's dead. Just get it out of here," Frank answered.

The sight of green blood was alarming but not enough to freak the men out. Otilia was just disgusted that she went to the bathroom to puke. After vomiting, she lost her appetite to eat anything. She couldn't get the sight of the dead mouse with green blood out of her head.

"Well, I know what I'm getting tomorrow," she told her husband.

"I'm sure they must have mouse traps in the supermarket. Where is the supermarket?" Ruben asked.

"It's down the block, just walk through the main road and there it is. You don't need a car to get there," Frank answered.

Once the three of them ate, they watched as the rain continued to fall. Frank saw it was time for him to head home. He said bye to Ruben and Otilia as he headed home. His house was only a couple of blocks away.

The couple decided that with the cool weather, it was a good idea to start putting stuff where it belonged. They fixed up the living room and their bedroom to start. Everything else could wait. After a long day, the couple was ready for bed.

They fell to bed rather quickly, hoping for a better day. The rain kept the house nice and cool.

Two o'clock in the morning, Otilia heard a strange noise from the kitchen. She was concerned that it might have been another mouse. Otilia didn't want to wake up her husband as he seemed tired. So she took a deep breath and got up to check. She put on her slippers and grabbed a bat from the hallway.

At first, she was worried it might have been a burglar. As she walked closer to the kitchen, the noise sounded like a small animal, not a human. She was relieved it wasn't a human but feared it might have been a mouse or even a rat.

She grabbed a flashlight from the ceramic floor. Turning on the light, she carefully looked for the source of the noise. When Otilia aimed her flashlight at the kitchen, she saw it was another mouse. Unlike the last one, this was an adult mouse. Otilia was scared but felt the need to eradicate the mouse before it could multiply.

She aggressively swung the bat at the mouse, only for it to get away from her. The mouse was still in the kitchen. Otilia panicked even more as she feared mice. Nonetheless, she figured she could scare off the mouse. This particular mouse didn't cower. Instead, it ran towards her slippers and started to bite into them.

Luckily the slippers weren't open toe, so the mouse wasn't biting into her flesh. Otilia was still scared. She tried to kick it off her, but the rodent held firm.

"This is no ordinary mouse. What the heck is it?" She asked herself.

With kicking proving to be a lost cause, Otilia took the bat and slammed the top of it onto the mouse, killing it. She breathed a sigh of relief as she sat on the floor. At the same time, she was disgusted by the sight of green blood.

"Oh no, not again!"

She rushed to the bathroom to puke some more. Ruben heard all the commotion and decided to check it out.

"Otilia, are you ok?" He asked her.

"No, there's another mouse in the kitchen that I killed," she answered.

"I don't see anything here."

"It was there. I swear I just killed it. There… it is…"

Otilia looked at the floor and saw the mouse was gone. Even the green blood was gone. She was stunned and scared. At that point, Otilia knew the house might have been infested with mice. Where there were mice, there had to be a rat.

"I don't see anything, mi amor."

"It was there! Look at my slipper."

"Listen, baby, I know you're a little scared because this is a new house in a quiet neighborhood."

"But…"

"But nothing. Once you get to know the neighborhood a bit better, you'll feel better and stop being so scared. Now come on, let's get some sleep."

Otilia wanted to believe her husband. However, her experience told a different story. It was one that only she knew of. She checked the bat and saw it had no blood on it, which stunned her.

"Dios mio! Que estan pasado?" She asked what was happening.

The first night at the 'dream house' proved to be a rough one.

Chapter 2

April 11th, 1985

The next morning, the couple got up. Otilia wanted to shake the memories of last night but couldn't. She was convinced there was something odd about the mice and the house. The so-called dream house had the makings of a total nightmare.

"What happened to the bread?" Ruben asked.

"See, there was a mouse in here!" Otilia felt vindicated.

"Perhaps you were right. However, I see a big bite mark on the bread. Are you sure it wasn't you?"

Otilia slapped her husband. She felt insulted that Ruben suggested that she could make a bite mark that big.

"Sorry... but it couldn't be a mouse."

"It might have been a rat."

"Cut it out Otilia! You know rats only exist in New York."

Otilia knew that what her husband was saying was bullshit. Rats loved the warm weather. She was concerned that the house was infested.

Looking outside, the couple saw that it was raining again. They were disappointed as the rain seemed to not want to leave Puerto Rico. Ruben heard the phone ring. He picked it up.

When he answered, it was the port in San Juan. His car had arrived on the island and he could pick it up.

"Good news, we're heading to San Juan today. The car is in the port," Ruben told his wife.

"Whew, it was about time. Call Frank so he can drive us there."

"Con calma, mi amor. It's still seven in the morning. Frank might not be awake yet. Although, I'm sure the weather in San Juan is probably better than here. Isn't it supposed to be the dry season?"

"Something is wrong with this place."

"The rain might be weird, but I'm sure things will normalize. As for the mice, you need to stop worrying about them."

Otilia wanted to believe Ruben. However, the signs were too hard to ignore. Out of nowhere, the two of them heard a loud screech.

Ruben got the bat and looked around the house, but nothing was around. Then he went to the yard and saw nothing. As much as he thought the quiet nature of the neighborhood would be a plus, Ruben was a bit fazed by how silent it was at his home. NYC was different. One could always find somebody if one needed something.

Even the streets were quiet. Not even a car could be seen driving by. What made it worst was that he lived on a dead-end road, which ensured traffic would be non-existent.

To his relief, there was nothing around the house. However, this time he heard the screech.

"See, nothing to be worried about," He did the best he could to hide the fear.

Looking to his right in the living room, he saw a baby mouse roaming around.

"Oh! There goes the little bastard!" Ruben shouted.

He rushed to it and swiped it with the broom, killing it. Unlike the previous mouse, the blood was red. Otilia was relieved at first. However, the last bit of blood to pour out was green.

"See, I got the little rascal!"

"But that was only a baby mouse. The mouse I saw was bigger and more aggressive. Also, why do I see green blood?" She asked.

"I wish I had an answer for that. However, I don't think we should bring it up when Frank takes us to get the car," Ruben answered.

"Why not?"

"No need for us to be scared during the car ride. Maybe the mice were sick."

Otilia wanted to believe that was a possibility. However, it was too much of a coincidence that the three dead mice all had green blood. Also, the few neighbors around were complaining about an uptick in mouse sightings. Not to mention, the mice were more aggressive and bled out green blood when killed. It wasn't all of the mice, but it was a significant amount. The fact that the neighborhood was silent didn't help her train of thought.

She feared that there was a posse of rats infesting the neighborhood. As for the green blood, Otilia feared that there was a virus going around. She only imagined what could happen if a human was bitten.

At the moment, she had to keep her fears to herself. Frank arrived at the house, ready to take the couple to the port.

The rain poured as they got into the car. As Otilia got in the car, she heard a loud screech coming from the house. She felt some relief as she headed out. The problem was that she would have to return home eventually. The only hope was that the mice she found were outliers, not the norm.

The weather in San Juan proved to be much sunnier than in the southern part of Puerto Rico. Frank and the others enjoyed a day out after getting Ruben's car.

When they got back to Salinas, the clouds were still there. The rain had calmed down quite a bit. The neighborhood was extremely quiet, a bit too silent for Otilia's good.

The neighbor that was in front of her was usually sitting outside. On this day, however, he wasn't. The door to the house was closed and so were the windows. Otilia and even Ruben found this to be a bit odd. Nonetheless, they arrived at their own home.

Upon entering, Otilia expected the worst. However, she saw that the house was spotless. It was the same way that she and her husband left it. She breathed a sigh of relief.

Otilia knew the real test would come at night. Everyone said their goodbyes as Frank went back to his house. The rain picked up in intensity again. Since the stove wasn't due until the next day, Ruben decided they should head out to eat. With a car, they could drive out themselves.

They ended up in a seafood restaurant. The restaurant was themed as a pirate ship. There were plenty of pirate themed items hung up including the Jolly Roger. It was a family friendly place that also suited couples.

There they ate a Dorado fish, which was native to the Caribbean Sea along with fried plantains. Along with the food, they both had delicious pina coladas to wash the fish down. After eating, Otilia felt better as she hadn't seen anything strange the whole day. There was a chance that things were going to get better.

As Ruben watched the television, he became encouraged when he saw the weather was forecasted to improve by late tomorrow. It was a bit of a rough start, but he felt things would turn.

After the two of them enjoyed their meal, they headed home.

Meanwhile in the outskirts of town…

A couple of farmers were finishing up for the day. There was a large farm of banana trees and plantains, both native to Puerto Rico. The increase in the rain helped the soil and ensured the plants had enough water to grow.

They enjoyed the weather, knowing the cooler weather wouldn't be as taxing to their bodies.

"Hermano, if only the weather could stay like this forever," one of the farmers said.

"Claro que si," the other farmer agreed.

On the horizon, a gang of rats was just outside the farm. These weren't regular rats, as their eyes were green. It wasn't just one, it was around a hundred rats.

The farmers had no idea that the hungry rats were nearby. Some of the plants were being eaten by the rats until all of the rats started to eat the banana trees.

One of the farmers looked behind him and saw the banana trees shrinking.

"Mida! Que estan pasado!" One of the farmers asked what was happening.

"No puede se! Algo estan comedio la pala de guineo!" The other farmer claimed that something was eating the banana tree.

Both farmers grabbed their rifles just in case it was a dangerous animal or an iguana they could kill and eat later on. They walked carefully to where the banana trees were. When they reached, they were horrified by their discovery.

"No! Son ratas!" One of the farmers screamed rats.

"Dios mio! Hay mucha ratas aqui!" His partner saw it wasn't just one rat but an army of them.

The two farmers started shooting at the rats with their rifles. They managed to kill a few of the rats. However, the numbers were too much. The rats charged at the farmers and overwhelmed them.

The rats dug into the flesh of the farmers, eating them mercilessly. The green eyes on the rats suggested they were not acting naturally at all. One of the farmers fell to the ground. The rats bit into his dead body as they ripped his chest apart. Also, they started to dig into his legs.

A loud sound was heard from the county road by those passing by. They had no idea that sound was the combined squeaks of about one-hundred rats prepared to take over the town of Salinas.

The other farmer fought off the rats as he tried to run away. However, he slipped on a rock and fell face-first. He quickly turned around to get back on his feet, but it proved to be a fruitless effort. The last thing he saw was the green eyes of the rats. The rodents looked hungry for blood.

Unlike the first farmer, the rodents took their time on their prey. Also, unlike the other farmer, they didn't gang up on him to eat him alive. Instead, three rats came up on him. One of them bit him on the leg, another on the arm, and the last on his neck.

While he survived the bites, the farmer knew he was a dead duck. Nonetheless, he tried to keep his cool, hoping the rodents would roam away.

A minute later, he felt a sharp pain in his heart. What he didn't know was that the rodent had infected him with venom.

The venom appeared to cause the rats to turn aggressive and deadly. Where the venom came from was anyone's guess.

The farmer screamed in pain until it was too much and perished. The rats started to bite and suck his blood. Unlike normal human blood, the blood of the farmer had turned green. The same color that Otilia had seen with the mouse she had killed.

Instead of biting the body, the rats were sucking his blood as if they were thirsty. The poor farmer lay on the ground dead as an army of rats had sucked him dry.

The rats finished up by eating the majority of the banana trees. The rumors of a rat infestation were coming true. Yet the town of Salinas was unaware.

Ruben and Otilia's Residence

The couple drove back home. Ruben parked his car in the driveway for the night. After a nice dinner, they were ready for bed. Otilia looked around and saw nothing unusual. They turned on the nightly news. Other than the normal news, there was nothing about the rat infestation in Salinas.

Otilia and Ruben were a bit calmer. They were excited for tomorrow as the sun was supposed to come back out. Before going to bed, they heard the sound of a mouse.

Unlike before, it was a mouse that fell into a glue trap. It was an adult-sized mouse that struggled to get out of the trap. The two didn't wait for it to die. Instead, they threw the mouse in the trash where it would perish. It was at this point that Otilia started to feel optimistic about things.

It was a rough start to their dream life in Puerto Rico, but it was bound to improve. The couple went to bed. They were able to sleep through the whole night without anything wrong. However, that feeling of security wouldn't last long.

Neither Otilia nor Ruben had any idea of the horrors that awaited them just a few miles away. The town of Salinas would be invaded by…

Rats!

Chapter 3

April 12th, 1985

The night for Otilia and Ruben passed. It was uneventful. More importantly, no mice were spotted. It was six in the morning. Otilia got up to use the bathroom. She was careful where she walked to.

Otilia looked on the floor for any rodents. To her surprise, there were none around. She breathed a sigh of relief as no mice were in the house. With no mice seen, she continued with her routine. She brushed her teeth and washed her hands. It was a typical start to the day.

Ruben was stuck in bed. He was too relaxed to get up right away. Not even the sound of running water was enough to wake him up.

As for Otilia, she finished using the bathroom. She looked outside and saw it was still cloudy, to her shock.

"Why is it still cloudy?" She asked herself.

The meteorologist called for sunny conditions for the day. Otilia wondered if the sun would come out. She hoped it would as it would cheer her up. The sun had yet to show up in Salinas. Nonetheless, she went on with her normal routine.

She heated some coffee. The aroma was refreshing. It had been a while since the last time she made homemade coffee. The smell of the perking coffee was pungent enough to reach the bedroom. Ruben smelled the coffee and got right up.

"Homemade coffee? About damn time. I was getting tired of getting it from the coffee shop," he said to himself.

Ruben got up from bed and headed to the bathroom. He looked outside and saw the sun wasn't out. He figured it was morning fog that would eventually burn away with the heat of the day. While it was cloudy, it wasn't raining.

There were puddles of rainwater still around. However, they started to evaporate. Ruben hoped he wouldn't see any more rain puddles. He was looking forward to the beach day.

The two of them enjoyed their coffee and toast. Even better, sunlight started to pop through the clouds. The couple was encouraged by the sun coming out. With the sun coming out, they were ready to gather their beach clothes.

Ruben got busy gathering the beach towels, chairs, and clothes they planned to take. As for Otilia, she made finger sandwiches, got some snacks, and got the ice ready to put into the cooler. She considered whether to call Frank to go with them or if it should have just been a couple's day out.

She didn't mind either way. All she wanted to do was enjoy herself. Things such as looking for a job would come later when they settled.

When she prepared everything, Otilia started to load everything in the car. She struggled to open the trunk since it had to be opened manually. Otilia was happy with the 1978 Chevy Camaro they had. However, she was ready for an upgrade. The 1985 Camaro was a beauty in her eyes. They had the money for an upgrade. Ruben was a cheapskate, however. He figured as long as their current car was still running, there was no need for an upgrade.

When she put the stuff in the trunk, Otilia noticed something off. She saw that the light on the trunk was off. Despite that, she didn't think much of it. When she closed the trunk door, Otilia heard a squeak.

She looked around but couldn't see anything. There were no signs of a mouse around. Nonetheless, she was cautious in her search. She even looked under the Camaro. It was all clear.

"It's probably in my head," she whispered.

She walked back into the house to check on her husband.

"Mi amor, todo bien?" She asked if everything was ok.

"Yes, baby. I'm ok," he answered.

Before packing the rest of the stuff in the car, Otilia went to the house across the street to check on her neighbor. It was a middle-aged couple who lived there. The husband and wife lived alone. They were in their lower fifties. The couple resided in Salinas well before the start-up neighborhood was constructed.

Otilia heard stories about the neighborhood being built on top of sugar cane farms.

The husband wasn't outside like he always was. Otilia found it a bit strange. She figured that they were at work already. Things were only stranger when she saw the front door open. She felt off walking into the house. Otilia was told by her neighbors to walk in if she felt something was off.

Taking a deep breath, she walked inside. Otilia investigated the house. The kitchen and living rooms seem to be in good shape. She heard some squeaking coming from the back. Before moving on, she checked the phone in case she needed to call the police or medics. When she picked up the rotary phone, it was silent. There was no dial tone. When she spun the dial, there was no tone on the phone. Otilia saw the phone line was cut.

However, the cut didn't look human in nature. There were bite marks on the wire.

"Mice were in here, so where are they?" She asked.

She was concerned, knowing there was no sign of life in the house. The bite marks looked like mice had cut the wire. She was no expert on rewiring a phone line.

Otilia walked back to the bedrooms. She hoped that her neighbors were oversleeping. When she reached the master bedroom, her jaw dropped.

"What happened?" She shouted.

Her neighbors were bleeding in bed, filled with bite marks. The bodies were completely torn apart. Otilia was terrified from the mutilated bodies and the blood splattered around the room. She was convinced that this wasn't caused by a human. Otilia didn't bother talking to them, as she knew they were both dead. There was no way neither of them would still be alive after being bitten alive.

Her fear was confirmed. Both of them were eaten alive by mice. The bite marks were those of rodents. She believed there were blood-sucking rats in the neighborhood. Next she looked outside and saw the sun blocked by dark gray clouds.

"So much for the weatherman..." she said.

The rain clouds were rushing through the neighborhood. Thunder was also heard as a rainstorm was doomed to arrive despite the weatherman saying otherwise. Otilia wasn't surprised by the inaccuracy of the weatherman. She was used to it back in New York.

She rushed back home to tell Ruben about her discovery. Downpours started to fall once again, to her dismay. When she got inside, Otilia put her rainboots on along with her cameo pants. Her plans for a relaxing day had taken a dark turn. She prepared to have to file a police report.

"There must be rats here... I must be prepared!" She said in her head.

"No! It's raining. I thought there was no rain today," Ruben shouted.

"Forget about the rain,"

"What's wrong? Why are you dressed like that and why do you look like you saw a ghost?"

"Baby, I went next door to check on our neighbors. They're dead!"

"What! How did they die?"

"They have mouse bites on them!"

"Oh, come on, you expect me to believe that? You and your mice..."

"We have to call the police to report this! There's no time to talk down to me."

"Ok, no problem, I'll call now. You check the car in case."

Otilia rushed to the car to get it started. When she got in, the car didn't start. She continued to try and start the vehicle. However, no lights lit up on the dashboard. She quickly opened the hood. The wiring leading to the battery was chewed up, to her shock.

"Crap, this car is done!" she shouted,

"The line is cut! We gotta go to the police station!" Ruben told his wife.

"No good! The wire to the battery is all chewed up. The car won't even start!"

As they saw their day turn around, they heard loud squeaks.

"Oh my god! What was that?" Ruben asked.

Otilia walked with Ruben to the back of the house, trying to reach for their handgun. It was no good. The back of the house was infested with large rats with green eyes. The rodents had been hiding under the bed and had a strong appetite for humans.

"I told you there were rats!" Otilia shouted.

Ruben foolishly attempted to go into the bedroom to obtain his handgun. Otilia tried to pull him back. He overpowered her and headed to the bedroom. The rats quickly rushed into the room and ate him up.

The screams were heard for Otilia to hear. Her husband had become breakfast for the hungry rats. As much as a gun would've helped her, she knew it was a foolish errand to go for the gun. In only a t-shirt, cameo pants, and rain boots, Oitlia ran out of her dream house.

The rats were seen overwhelming the house, eating everything they could get their hands on. Her greatest fear was now a reality. She ran as fast as she could without a car or even access to a phone. The best hope for her was to find a pay phone and get the cops involved. She feared that even the cops would not be enough to take on this new threat.

The rain was falling heavily. Otilia could care less about getting wet. This was all about survival at this point. She hoped the rats weren't chasing her, but she couldn't stop running. The only place she knew where there was a payphone was the supermarket.

What was supposed to be a beach day had turned into a nightmare. The neighborhood was infested with rats.

Chapter 4

The rain continued to pour on Salinas. What was a quiet and small neighborhood was now infested with the demon-like rats. Otilia was stunned that she could not go back home. She wanted to cry non-stop after seeing her husband murdered by the rodents. However, there was no turning back.

This was now a matter of survival. The rats were still in her house, enjoying eating whatever was there. She was a safe distance from the murderous horde of rodents.

Without a car, her only choice was to head to Frank's house. The hope was that the rats had not reached his house. The sun was completely gone. It had turned into a dark day with heavy rain. Also, the temperatures were stuck in the low 70s. Once again, the weather was abnormal for Salinas.

On a typical day, temperatures should have climbed well into the 80s. However, on this day, temperatures were plummeting. Otilia felt cold despite living in NYC for a few years. The rain and high winds made it even chillier.

There was no time to get anything warm. All she could do was run to Frank's house. The neighborhood was quiet, as it was still seven in the morning. She screamed, hoping to get the attention of everyone in the block. An elderly lady came out and screamed at her.

The old lady was wearing her nightgown still. She had white hair and looked to be in her upper 70s. She seemed to be in good health as she was walking normally.

"Que tu ase! Esta loca?" The lady accused Otilia of being crazy.

"Hay Ratas y va a matar a nosotros!" Otilia tried to convince the woman of the killer rats.

The old lady laughed at Otilia. She truly believed that Oitlia had lost her mind.

"Adios loca! Por favor, vete, ante que yo llamar la policia!" The old lady wasn't interested in Otilia's story.

Otilia prepared to leave but saw a large rat behind the lady. She panicked as she saw the green eyes on the rat.

"Que paso ahora. Tu eres loca de verdad!" The elderly lady told Otilia.

"Rata!" That was all Otilia could muster up.

The woman turned around and saw the rat. Her face turned white when she saw that Otilia was right about the rats. She grabbed a broomstick and slapped the rat away from her. The rat didn't crawl away like a normal rat.

Instead, it growled and ready to pounce on the woman. Otilia felt bad running away but was unarmed. Also, she had no idea if there were any more rats nearby. After all, if there was one rodent, there were bound to be more of them. She needed to protect herself.

The rat jumped in the face of the woman and started to bite her. The woman didn't give in easily. She grabbed the rat and slammed it to the ground. Otilia heard a loud squeak from the rat.

"Whoa, this woman is tough! She might be helpful," she said to herself.

Any hope of befriending the lady quickly went by the wayside as she saw more rats rushing the lady. Despite her toughness, the elderly lady was no match for the horde of twenty rats. The rodents showed no mercy eating the poor lady alive. They took large bites into her flesh like it was cheese. The old lady was torn apart like it was fresh meat. It was too much for Otilia to watch as she ran from the scene.

There was no time to waste. Otilia needed to reach Frank. He lived a couple of blocks from her. She slipped on a large puddle and fell face first. The fall hurt quite a bit as she fell on her knees. There was no time to lick her wounds. Behind her, the horde of rats only grew larger and closer. Along with that, the squeaks grew louder. If anybody in the neighborhood was unaware of the rat infestation they were either oblivious or dead.

Otilia got up from the puddle. Her cameo pants were all wet, along with her pink T-Shirt. At least the rain boots kept her feet dry. She would have to dig into her country background. Back in El Salvador, she grew up in the country. She was familiar with farming and living without technology. Also, she was used to getting injured during her farming background.

She pushed herself through the driving rain until she reached Frank's house. When she got there, she saw Frank through the window. He had a baseball bat. Frank was swinging it at a couple of rats who broke into his house. Otilia couldn't bare to see her friend struggle.

The front door was open. A stick was by the door. She grabbed it and rushed into Frank's house. Frank was shocked but happy to see Otilia.

"What are you doing here? Get out of here before they get you!" Frank shouted.

"I'm here to save you from the rats. Come on! If we work together, we can survive!" Otilia retorted.

Otilia swung her stick at the rats, which lunged in her direction. Frank would do the same. The two of them worked together to kill off the rats. The living room was splattered with green blood. The sight was quite disgusting. At the very least, Otilia had saved Frank from being eaten alive.

"Thank you for saving me. Que paso con Ruben?" Frank asked where Ruben was.

"Este muerto, las ratas lo mato," she told Frank that the rats had killed her husband.

"No puede se. It can't be. Where did these little fuckers come from?"

"I have no idea, Frank. The only thing I know is that we need to get going. It's not safe in our homes. Now I know why the local politicians were against building the homes over the farmland."

"Now we won't have sugar," Frank said in a discouraged tone.

"Are you stupid? You over here worried about sugar. Meanwhile, the rats have taken over the neighborhood!" Otilia said as she slapped Frank.

"What do we do now? My car is busted. Those rodents ate the battery cable. My car is dead on the road."

"So is mine. All we can do is head to the supermarket across the main road. We'll find plenty of shelter there. Also, we might be able to gather needed goods. More importantly, there's bound to be a payphone there."

"Why do we need a payphone for?"

"Oh, Frank, do I need to have all the answers? It's so we can call the cops!"

"What are the cops going to do?"

"They can hold the rats back. Since they're an authority figure, they might get the national guard to get us out of here."

"I have to say bye to Salinas?"

"Unless you want to die next to your coconut tree, then yes."

Frank nodded his head. He realized that Otilia was correct. His wife passed away a couple of years ago. However, he wasn't ready to join her in the afterlife just yet.

"Get some comfortable clothes. You'll need it. Also, can I borrow a sweater of yours?" She asked.

"Sure... besides, it's not like I'll be coming back here anytime soon," he answered.

Frank handed Otilia one of the old sweaters that he hated wearing. What they wore wasn't important. This was purely about survival.

The two of them gathered any other supplies they saw useful. A book of matches and a flashlight were good items for them to take. As they left Frank's house, a couple of rats entered through the front door.

They kept their cool as they swung their weapons at the rats. Otilia impaled the rat before it could get up. She held the urge to vomit when the green blood came out of the rat's body.

As for Frank, the rat grabbed onto the end of his baseball bat. He swung the bat into the wall, where he slammed the rat. Frank continued to bash the rat into the concrete wall until it squeaked. When it squeak, green blood came out of its body. His house was filled with green blood.

While Otilia held in the urge to puke, Frank was unable to.

"Would you get going? We have to get out of here!" Otilia hurried Frank.

"Sorry, I needed to get that out of my system."

As both of them left the home, they saw a horde of rats climbing a palm tree. The rats jumped onto a power pole. When they got on the pole, they chewed on the power cable. The transformer blew up, scaring Frank and Otilia to death.

"You gotta be kidding me! Let's get out of here!" Frank freaked out.

"Thought you were never ask!" Otilia replied.

The two ran from the house, not wanting to be near the rat horde. They hoped the supermarket would be a safe haven.

Meanwhile

Plenty of people were seen in the supermarket, going about their normal day. There was one man who was unlike the others.

A bald man with a big beard was walking around the supermarket. Everyone gave him a weird look, not knowing what he was up to. What made him even more out of place was his Miami Dolphins jersey. It was a Dan Marino jersey.

American football wasn't a thing in Puerto Rico. There were a few football fans on the island, but they were mostly ex-patriots. Baseball was the bigger sport on the island. Nobody in the supermarket knew who the dolphins were. The only thing that jersey told the residents was that he was an American from the US mainland.

His name was Jack. He wasn't Puerto Rican, not even close. He was from Gallatin, Tennessee. It was a humble town filled with wonderful people, who welcomed outsiders with open arms. It was similar to Salinas when it came to being welcoming. Jack had the look of someone from Tennessee.

He was a huge football and baseball fan. However, he wasn't here to watch any games. Heck, he wasn't even there for vacation. Jack was a bounty hunter. His code name was Wolf. He was hired to go after a notorious criminal in Puerto Rico with ties to Tennessee. His name was Gustavo.

Gustavo was a drug dealer and involved with many fraud operations in Puerto Rico and the Gallatin area. Jack was hired to investigate and bust him. He enjoyed cashing in on private bonds and kickbacks to capture criminals. That was despite the numerous legal liabilities since he wasn't a police officer or detective.

Since he wasn't a legal officer, Jack had to rely on a skip. A skip was a term used by hunters to find a person's whereabouts. Jack relied on outside contacts such as stalkers, journalists, and even repossession agents.

When it came to Gustavo, Jack had to rely on a repossession agent he knew in Puerto Rico. It seemed that Gustavo had a couple of cars in Salinas that were up for repossession. The plan was to use the info to find and bust Gustavo.

Jack hoped to catch Gustavo since he needed the money to pay for the trip to and from Puerto Rico. Also, he was saving up to buy his mother a house.

He looked around and stood around. Jack figured that Gustavo would come to the supermarket at some point. This was the biggest supermarket in Salinas. Mostly everyone in town came here to shop. Salinas was still underdeveloped, so this was the only place to go unless one wanted to drive an hour away to the next town of Santa Isabel.

Jack didn't know much about Puerto Rico. He hoped it was a quick operation where he didn't have to go on a wild goose chase around the island. Jack was in the supermarket for a while, but there was no sign of Gustavo.

As he walked through the meat aisle, he heard squeaking. Jack looked around and didn't see anything. He thought it was a mouse but saw nothing. He was getting hungry, so he figured he would stop off at the deli section to grab a bacon and egg sandwich. The man behind the counter spoke good English, so Jack wasn't worried.

As Jack ordered his sandwich, he saw a couple of large rats behind the man. His appetite all of a sudden went away. The rats had green eyes just like the ones that Otilia had seen. Jack had no idea these were killer rats.

When he told the man to cancel the order Jack heard a scream.

"What the hell was that?" Jack asked.

"I don't know," the worker answered.

"I reckon I better check it out. It might be a female giving birth," Jack said.

Jack walked toward the middle of the supermarket, trying to find the source of the screaming. As he walked around, he saw more rats roaming around.

"This place has a rat problem. Luckily I don't live here, seesh," he said to himself.

When he looked around in the cookie aisle, he saw a couple of people being eaten by rats. Jack was shocked by the sight of the blood-sucking rats. He rushed to the cleaning supply aisle and saw a woman getting her blood sucked by the rats.

"What the fuck is this? This is something straight out of a movie. I had no idea mice could be so freaking deadly!"

He heard gunfire and figured it might have been Gustavo. Jack didn't want to miss his chance to capture the suspect. He rushed toward the noise. A few rats attempted to lunge at him. Jack shot them with his handgun.

When he turned around, Jack saw more rats entering through the ventilation system. That is when he realized this was no regular rodent infestation.

He rushed toward the noise. While catching Gustavo was paramount, this was turning into a mission of survival. Jack saw a couple of National Guard members lying dead on the floor. There were armed with machine guns. He felt wrong taking one of them but needed to survive.

Jack turned around and emptied a clip at a horde of rats that were behind him. He grabbed a couple of clips from the dead bodies.

Jack continued into the manager's office upstairs, hoping to find a safe place to hide. Also, he looked for a phone to use. When Jack got to the manager's office, he found the phone was dead. The phone line was bitten in half.

"God damnit! I better get out of here. There's bound to be more rats in this consumer hell hole," Jack said.

Jack also found Gustavo. He was bummed, though. Gustavo was on the floor, dead. The criminal was bitten to death by the invading rats.

"There goes my payday, for fuck sake. What else can go wrong here?" Jack angrily asked.

The only thing Jack had to be concerned about was survival.

Back in the neighborhood

Otilia and Frank walked toward the corner across the street from the strip mall where the supermarket was. There was no light, so they had to watch carefully for traffic. There was no traffic to speak of. So they crossed the main road rather easily.

They had no idea that even the supermarket was no safer than where they were. The rats had taken over the town and their population was only growing.

Chapter 5

Otilia and Frank had just finished crossing the main road. The rain continued to fall in earnest. At this point, neither of them worried about getting wet. They knew that survival was the name of the game. They approached the local coffee shop and it wasn't to get coffee.

The hope was to find a survivor, such as a police officer. If not, finding a working phone was the next best thing. It was silent as they walked into the coffee shop. They heard some squeaking, but it was coming from a distance.

"We might be safe here," Frank said.

"Perhaps, but it won't be for long. Those rats are hungry. They'll be here soon," Otilia replied.

When they entered the coffee shop, it was eerily silent. Usually around this time, the shop would be bustling with freshly baked bread and perking coffee. This was Frank's favorite place to come in the morning. On this day, it was anything but welcoming.

They carefully walked through the shop, not knowing if any rats were inside. A loud bang was heard from the back. Otilia quickly turned around with her stick engaged. However, she saw nothing ahead.

"It must have been a pot. Somebody must be here," Frank whispered.

The two of them were convinced somebody was inside. They hoped whoever was inside was alive and just hiding. As they walked further back, they saw green blood on the wall.

"Oh no, they were here. The rats were here," she told Frank.

"You're right. Hopefully, we find a survivor to help us out. Follow me, I know the owner of this place. He might be of some help to us," Frank replied.

They had to be even more careful as there was evidence of rats in the establishment. Frank opened the double doors slowly. He peeked inside and saw the coast was clear. Otilia followed him into the kitchen. For a coffee shop, the kitchen was huge.

There was a machine that made fresh bread along with many stoves. It was silent as no machine was operational. The trail of green blood extended into the kitchen.

"I'm a bit worried. Look at the time. It's nearly eight o'clock. It shouldn't be this silent. Something is terribly wrong," Frank felt something was off.

"You would think there would be a police officer getting coffee," Otilia told Frank.

"Exactly, it's just silent. We have to investigate and leave. I don't think it's a smart idea to stay in here. For all we know, there might already be rats in here."

When the two walked deeper into the kitchen, they heard a scream from the manager's office. The two of them rushed towards the office. They tried to open the door, but it was locked. Frank figured the owner was inside, so he kicked the door. The door opened as the lock broke off.

Rats were spotted eating the owner. Frank and Otilia barged in and started to attack the rats with their weapons. One of the rats nearly bit Frank, but he slapped the rat away from him. There were mouse traps that proved ineffective against the super rats.

One of the rats attempted to ambush Frank from behind. Otilia intercepted the rat and slapped it with her broomstick. The rat flew to the other side of the room and struck the wall hard. The impact was enough to kill the rat. There were still three more rats in the room.

Otilia and Frank got in front of the injured owner to protect him. The rats crawled closer with their evil green eyes staring at them. Otilia knew she would have to get over her fear of rodents quickly. Green blood came out of the mouths of the giant rats.

The rats went on the attack and lounged at Frank and Otilia. One of the mice landed on Frank's arm. It managed to bite him. He shook off the rodent before it could bite him any deeper. Another rat tried to lounge at his feet. He kicked it away with his feet. When the rat landed, he impaled it repeatedly with the tip of the bat until it was dead.

Otilia rushed to the other rat that was down. She struck the rat with her stick with a few pokes until the green blood splattered out of its body. Some of the blood got onto her. It wasn't anything that couldn't be washed away easily.

There was one more rat in the office. The two of them double-teamed the rat and killed it easily. They looked around for any more rodents. The coast was clear as no more rats came into the room. They even checked the ventilation shaft for anything and found it was clear.

"Que paso, Carlos? Estan bien?" Frank asked.

"No... hermano. Yo puedo mucho sangre. Yo voy por lo cielo pronto," the shop owner claimed he was dying as he lost too much blood.

"No dice eso! Tu eres furete. Este ratas no van a ganar a nosotros," Frank tried to convince Carlos that he couldn't give up.

The reality was that Carlos had lost a lot of blood due to being bitten multiple times. His bites were deep as well. There was no denying that no amount of motivation would help Carlos. Nonetheless, Frank got a cloth to use as a tourniquet to stop Carlos from losing too much blood.

As Frank was helping the owner, he felt a sharp pain in his right arm. Also, he was losing blood from the wound. Otilia jumped into action. She was a medic back in El Salvador, helping the government soldiers during the civil war there. She got a piece of cloth to cover up Frank's wound.

Unlike Carlos' wound, Frank's injury was easy to cover. After helping Frank, Otilia gave him a hand with Carlos.

"Gracias par ayudame. Pero, es muy tarde. Ese ratas va a matar todo lo gente," Carlos said it was too late, that the rats would take everyone out.

"Oh man, he's losing too much blood, even with the tourniquet. I don't know if we can save him," Otilia gave the grim diagnosis.

"We can't give up, though!" Frank said emotionally.

Carlos was like a second father to Frank. Carlos stepped up as a father figure when his father died in a freak hiking accident. He didn't want to lose him.

"Hijo, es muy tarde para me. Pero, to puede salvar tu mismo. Dejame, tu tiener mucho para vivar todavia. Te quiero mucho, hijo. Adios..." Carlos said his last words before passing away. He loved Carlos like a son but knew he needed to move on. His wounds were too much to overcome.

Frank cried when Carlos passed away. Otilia did her best to comfort him. She hugged him. While she never knew Carlos, she understood that to Frank, he was his world. Otilia had a flashback of when her first boyfriend was killed during the civil war in El Salvador. So she understood losing somebody close.

"I'm so sorry..."

"Thanks, hun. He was like a father to me. He took care of me when my father passed away. He died during a hiking accident in the mountains. My first job was cleaning the shop and helping him pack stuff. This shop has been here for close to twenty years," he replied.

"I can tell you loved him."

"I did... As he said, however, we have to move on. He's in a better place. We on the other hand, still have to deal with this hell. It's not safe here. We have to get going."

"Yes, we do, but can we try the phone here?"

Frank nodded. Otilia picked up the phone in the office and saw it was dead. She checked the wire but saw it wasn't bitten or chewed.

"How can that be? The wire seems to be ok," Otilia asked.

"Damn, I think the rats might have started to eat the wires coming from the main line. If that's the case, we might be screwed."

"Does that mean we're doomed to die in this hell hole?"

"No... it just means if we want help, we're going to have to travel to find it. If we only had a car. Wait, the supermarket has its dedicated phone line. We might be in luck if we head there."

"It's worth a try. It's better than staying here to get bit by rats. Are you ok with your arm?"

"You did a fine job. I can barely feel anything. Then again, that rat couldn't get its teeth into my flesh."

The two of them walked out of the coffee shop. Frank knew it would never be the same ever again. It was tough saying bye to a family friend.

Without a car, the supermarket was the best destination to head to. It was a short five-minute walk. Otilia looked behind her and saw the rats on the other side of the road. Time was running out. The two of them needed to get help. The rodents were only getting closer to overrunning the town of Salinas.

The rain lightened up just a bit, which was a relief for Otilia and Frank. There were many puddles on the ground. However, their vision would improve as the rain wasn't in their eyes. There were no rats as they made the trek to the supermarket. What they did notice was the absence of people. Not everyone took their car to the market.

However, they did see the parking lot filled with plenty of cars.

"Ah, cars! I think we might have hit the jackpot. There's bound to be survivors inside," Frank said.

"Not to mention, a working phone," Otilia said, encouraged.

There was one thing that discouraged him. While there were cars, there was a lack of foot traffic. Nobody was walking in or out of the supermarket.

"What's wrong?" Otilia asked.

"I think we're wrong about the supermarket being safe," he answered.

"What makes you say that?"

Frank didn't answer right away. He wanted to get closer to the market before making any observations.

When the two of them got closer, his suspicion was correct.

"I want you to answer this. What do you see that is off?" He asked.

"It seems normal to me."

"Look again. I want you to focus."

Otilia took a better look and saw no traffic coming in or out of the supermarket.

"The people... there's no people around."

"That is correct. I have a horrible suspicion that our enemy has already beaten us here. We might be too late. Despite that, we don't have much of a choice but to explore."

Otilia nodded as the two of them walked into the supermarket. When they walked it, the lights were still on. However, it was silent. There was no music playing in the background. It was ghostly silence. There were no signs of people either. They feared that whatever people were inside were already slaughtered.

The first thing Otilia saw was the payphones.

"Look, payphones!" She said.

"I'll check it out," Frank replied.

Frank walked to the three phones. Two payphones were rotary, while the third was an upgraded touch-tone phone. It was part of the modernization plan for Salinas.

He tried all of the phones. To no surprise, the quarter was spat back out. None of the phones were operational. The sound of a dial tone was non-existent.

"Well, I only wished phones worked without dial tone because these phones are as silent as this hell hole," Frank said.

"No! You mean the rats have beaten us here?"

"I'm afraid so... These little bastards have become quite the menace. Sadly, they have the upper hand over us. All we can do is gather whatever supplies we can get our hands on and go on the road."

"You mean we're going to have to walk?"

"Sadly so, hun. Unless we're lucky enough to find a car not eaten by rats, our feet will have to do. Ughh, I wish I had better news, but that's how the cookie crumbles."

Otilia accepted her fate. The two of them started to explore what they could find in the supermarket. Without a car, they wouldn't be able to take much. For starters, they each had a drink of water. Without a cashier, there wasn't a point in not stealing the water.

They headed for the emergency supplies aisle. Over there would be some useful things for the road. When they reached the aisle, they heard squeaks.

"Oh, come on, not here!" Otilia whined.

"Sadly so. There's plenty of cheese here, so I imagine they are attracted to this place." Frank responded.

When they turned to their right, there were a couple of rats ready to attack. They teamed up to kill the rats easily. A rat broke through the candles on the racks. It got onto Otilia, prepared to tear her neck. She grabbed it and slammed it down on the floor. She finished it off with her broomstick.

The two of them didn't see any more rodents, so they continued to explore what to take. When they walked deeper, they saw three corpses on the floor. There was a large pool of blood surrounding the dead bodies.

"God have mercy! They got torn apart. What the hell is this?!" Frank was in disbelief.

Otilia had to hold in the urge to vomit. She knew the sight was horrible. Before they could react, they saw rats coming from both directions. The horde was huge.

"Oh no, we can't fight all those!" Otilia panicked.

"You're right. This might just be the end," Frank said somberly.

"No, we can't go like this!"

The rats closed in on their prey. All they could see was a delicious meal in front of them, ready to enjoy. Frank and Otilia held hands, preparing to say their last goodbyes. The rats went on the attack.

"No!" Otilia screamed, hoping for a miracle.

Machine gun fire was heard. The mystery man shot up all of the rats with ease. The rats who prepared to eat Frank and Otilia were dead in a matter of seconds.

Otilia looked and saw it was Jack.

"Who are you? Thank you for saving us!" Otilia told Jack.

"You're not from here, are you?" Frank asked.

"No, but I'm glad I was here. I was able to save two people. I reckon that makes us teammates. Before I go any further, my code name is Wolf, but you can call me Jack," Jack introduced himself. He had a strong Southern accent.

"I'm Otilia and I just moved here."

"My name's Frank. Thank you for saving us. What brings you to Salinas, Puerto Rico?"

"I'm not supposed to say anything, but my mission is already compromised. So, I might as well come clean. I'm a bounty hunter."

"Hmm, sounds cool. Who you were trying to catch?"

"You might have heard of him. Here's a picture of him. His name is Gustavo Santiago."

"Oh yes, I know that cunt. He's a drug dealer here in Salinas. A huge one. You don't look Puerto Rican. How did you know about Gustavo?"

"I'm from Tennessee, so you're right about me not knowing jack shit about Puerto Rico, no pun intended. However, Gustavo has been doing business in my hometown of Gallatin, Tennessee. So as a bounty hunter, I figured to take the job and use that as an excuse to take a trip to this beautiful island. Sadly, it seems these rats were my welcoming committee."

"Do you have an idea where these rats are coming from, Jack?" Otilia asked.

"I wish. I don't even have much knowledge about the island of Puerto Rico. Your guess is as good as mine."

"I didn't think I would ever meet a Southerner here. Welcome to Puerto Rico. I only wished it was under better circumstances," Frank said as he shook Jack's hand.

"Thanks, man. That makes us partners. You owe me for saving you. Now that my mission is no longer relevant, I'm ready to leave this island," Jack replied.

"What happened to that good-for-nothing bastard, Gustavo?"

"The rats made dinner out of him. It's crazy to believe that some people in Tennessee, at least those in the countryside enjoy roasting these bastards to eat. I'm not that much of a hillbilly. I never tried eating roasted rat. Now how about we get out of this consumerist hell hole, shall we?" Jack asked.

"I thought you would never ask," Otilia said.

"Do you have a car, Jack?"

"Oh yes, in the parking lot. It's a rental jeep, but it'll do the trick. Let's hope that the rodents haven't at the car up."

"Oh, please no. A car is our best shot to escape or get anywhere on this island," Otilia hoped.

"Well then, partners, let's not rest on our laurels," Jack told the two.

The three of them teamed up, ready to escape the rat-infested supermarket. It was two regular joes and a bounty hunter from Tennessee. It was about the biggest set of misfits that could be created, but it was all about survival at this point.

Chapter 6

Otilia never thought getting her dream house in Puerto Rico would be such a nightmare. She had lost her husband in one false swoop. The reality of not being able to return home also killed her. Solving the financial impacts of her house being destroyed by the rats would have to come later. At the moment, it was all about survival.

She and Frank followed Jack around the supermarket. Still, in the emergency supplies aisle, everyone gathered needed supplies. The best pickups were batteries, flashlights, and matches. At the same time, they made sure to stock up on plenty of trail mix and peanuts. Much of Salinas was in the dark, so the survivors had to grab non-perishable items.

There was still power in the supermarket. With that in mind, everyone headed to the fridge. Water was the big ticket item. They each drank a bottle of water to keep themselves hydrated. At the same time, they took another bottle of water with them.

"Make sure you all get what you need. I got a feeling we won't be returning here," Jack instructed the others.

"I wish we could take the entire supermarket," Otilia replied.

"Same here... it's time to get out of here. I can tell this place is about to be unsuitable for camping out," Frank said.

"Why do you say that? What makes you think it's any better outside?" Jack asked.

"Look around you, pal! This place is completely dead. It can only sustain itself for so long before it rots, just like everything else around this hell hole. Besides, if we stay here, we're on our own," Frank answered.

"You think it'll be any safer outside in all that rain? It's not like you can hunt unless you plan to feed yourself with iguanas. The pickup truck I have is not in the best of shape either. Dude, you might want to think," Jack grilled Frank.

"I don't want to argue with you but take a deeper look around you. Nobody is working in the supermarket. We can't just camp out here forever. The food will eventually run out and spoil,"

"Wait a minute, Frank. Jack might have a point," Otilia said.

"See?" Jack intervened.

"There's plenty of food around here. As long as we kill any rats that enter, we can shelter," Otilia told Frank.

"This is a supermarket. Where are we going to get ammo for Jack's gun? And that's only the tip of the iceberg. Who the heck is coming here? Did you forget, there's no phone service here! Not to mention, the rats are very smart bastards. They might ambush us one by one. This is a huge building. Those rats can appear anywhere and it'll be impossible to detect where. Finally, who knows how much longer this place will have power?" Frank tried to instill common sense into Otilia and Jack.

"Jack and I don't know anything about this island. You expect us to get around?" Otilia retorted.

"That's fine. I can lead the way. All I'm saying is that staying here is a trap," Frank responded.

"Ok bro, we'll play this your way. However, let's stick around to make sure we're filled. Also, we'll need a plan of where we can run to. I'm not saying you're wrong. Eventually, the ultimate objective has to be escape. We just have to be smart about it," Jack calmed down to explain.

"I can live with that. A plan is a smart idea. Ok, guys, let's go to the manager's office," Frank said.

Jack was armed with the machine gun. He also had his handgun. Jack figured that someone else should hold his handgun in case any rats appeared.

"Who here knows how to use a gun?" He asked.

"I do... I experienced the civil war back in El Salvador," Otilia answered.

"Cool, you hold on to my gun. It might come in handy," Jack handed Otilia his sidearm.

He had an extra magazine. That was all, though.

The three of them walked until they reached the manager's office. When they got close, a small army of rats was by the door.

They waited for their next victim to eat up. The glowing green eyes were hard to miss.

"Oh, come on! Not these bastards again!" Frank shouted.

"Don't panic now. Get ready to fire!" Jack retorted.

The rats were determined to attack the crew. Jack and Otilia fired their weapons at the rats. They killed most of the rodents except for a couple. One of the rats lounged at Jack. Frank saw Jack having to reload his machine gun. With his bat, he intercepted the rat as he swung at it.

He made perfect contact with the large rat. The impact caused the rodent to fly toward the wall. The rat died immediately after impact. Frank took a deep breath.

"Wow, that was a great swing. You sure you never played professional baseball?" Jack was impressed.

"No, never played professionally, but I do play in the local league here in Salinas. I tend to believe that I'm pretty good," Frank answered while he winked.

Otilia saw the last rat rush back, trying to attack Frank from behind. Armed with Jack's handgun, she alerted Frank.

"Frank, behind you!" She shouted.

Frank looked at saw the rat lounging at him. He put his hands up, bracing for impact. There was little time for him to react.

Out of nowhere, Otilia dives to her right and shoots two rounds at the rat in mid-air. Both bullets strike the rat, killing it. The green blood was all around the supermarket. At this point, Otilia was starting to get over her fear of the green blood. She wasn't necessarily enjoying the adventure. Otilia just accepted that she needed to use her survival skills.

"That's some fine shooting there, gal. Woo!" Jack was impressed with Otilia's skill.

"As I said, I know how to survive. This chica isn't totally lost," she replied, winking back at Jack.

"I'm impressed. You don't look like a woman who uses a gun," Jack was still shocked.

"Looks can fool... I don't show my true self to everyone," she responded. Otilia gave Jack a friendly slap to the face.

Before the trio could get comfortable, the lights started to flicker.

"What the fuck!" Jack said.

"It's what I feared... the rats have caught up to the power supply to the market," Frank answered.

"Oh no... I guess Frank is right. We can't stay here," Otilia said, feeling discouraged.

"I guess... I have to agree. With no power, it's become too dangerous to stay here. Damn..." Jack said somberly.

"I know it's scary. I honestly don't know what to expect out of the elements. One thing I know is we can't stay here any longer. Besides, the power going out only gives up more incentive to get the hell out of here. Are you ready?" Frank asked.

"Not really, but we don't have much of a choice, do we? I reckon not." Jack answered reluctantly.

Otilia nodded her head in agreement. They made the tough decision leave the relative safety of the supermarket. Ironically, it was because it was no longer safe to be inside.

They would have to take the chance by going on the road. However, it was a necessary risk. Without phone service in the market, no one could be summoned for help. They all made their way back outside without incident. The rain had dwindled into a drizzle, which was perfect for the crew.

"Man, we didn't come up with much of a plan. Where do we go from here?" Jack asked.

"There's a police station not too far from here. The policemen might be able to help us. There's a station by the beach. We'll go to that one because I'm sure the station by the town center is already infested. I trust that the rats haven't reached the beach yet. That should give us enough time to gather any more survivors and perhaps come up with a better plan," Frank answered.

"Lead the way, bro," Jack told Frank.

Frank didn't reply. He asked Jack to lead them to his pickup. Jack's pickup truck was not too far from where they were. The vehicle was not in the best of condition, but it was the best Jack could get.

Jack's rental truck had quite a few fenders and bumps. It was a 1978 Chevy C10 pickup. While it wasn't all that good, it was in working condition. That was paramount. Jack opened the door to the truck. There was enough room in the front for the three of them to sit.

When Jack got in, Otilia and Frank prayed that the truck started. The motor of the truck started when Jack turned the key to the relief of everyone.

"Whew, the rats didn't get to the truck. That already increases the chance of survival. By the way, let me drive. I know how to get to the police station," Frank told Jack.

"It's all yours," Jack happily let Frank drive.

Frank drove the truck out of the parking lot and back onto the main road. The main road in Salinas was county road 3. The road was the west to east artery that led from Ponce to the southeastern part of the island.

They drove onto the main road heading east until they hit the traffic light. At the light, Frank turned right onto Route 181. This particular route was the main road that allowed travelers to go from southern Salinas to the northern, more mountainous portions.

The police station was south of where they were. Frank drove a half mile down Route 181 until he reached an intersection. Turning left was the only option if one wasn't heading straight. The alternative road was the gastronomy route. This road led tourists through some of the finest restaurants in Salinas and even all of Puerto Rico.

The restaurants varied from BBQ places to snack areas. Salinas was most popular for seafood. The tasty Dorado fish was the signature fish of the town. People from all over the island would come down to eat the delicious fish. It was also a fish sought after by the local fishermen.

Frank turned left without any issue, as traffic was non-existent. It was a surreal sight as he drove down the scenic gastronomy road. Even at this time of the morning, it was full, with businesses opening up. Some restaurants had a breakfast menu. Tourists were usually already out, but not on this day. In fact, there were a few dead bodies on the side of the road. It was a grueling sight to see on a beach route.

They passed by some of the restaurants. Otilia was admittedly hungry when Frank was driving by. Some beautiful homes were near the beach. Everyone wanted a house by the water, but there was a limited amount of property for sale.

Unlike the northern part of Salinas, the beach seemed to be untouched. Although, the crew spotted dead bodies not long ago. Frank didn't concern him with that. He focused on reaching the police station. Jack wished that he had come to Puerto Rico during more peaceful times. The sights were beautiful if one took away the circumstances.

After a few minutes, the three of them had reached the police station.

"What do we do here?" Jack asked.

"First, we hope there are survivors. I have a family friend who's a police officer. Hopefully, we meet her. We can use any help we can get," Frank answered.

At first, everyone was encouraged to see the police station standing. There was no sight of any blood or dead bodies. As they entered, that encouragement died out.

"It's empty..." Jack said.

"No puede se! Esta vacio!" Frank shouted.

"What did he say?" Jack asked Otilia.

"Sorry, I'll spell it out for you. This place is utterly deserted!" Frank answered angrily.

"Puedo como... why? Otilia asked.

"Did the 'rats' reach here?" Jack asked.

"They might of... We have to check further. Let's see if Martha is here. That's my friend who's a cop here," Frank replied.

The three of them walked into the two-story police station. Frank thought that the police might have been alerted already to what was happening. However, there was nobody there. Echoes were heard when everyone spoke.

The first floor was mostly holding cells for suspects. Everyone followed Frank into the holding cells. Most of the cells were empty except for one. The one that was filled contained a dead male.

He had tattoos, but they were barely noticeable due to the pool of blood covering them. Otilia was terrified of the discovery. His throat was torn apart as well. There was a hole on the back wall on the cell. That suggested the rats had broken into the police station.

Jack saw a locked door with a sign stating it was an armory. He decided to start picking the lock. Frank turned to see Jack doing the deed.

"What the hell are you doing?" Frank asked.

"We need more ammo. We don't know how long we're going to be on the road." Jack answered.

"This is a police station! Come on, have a bit more respect," Frank retorted while slapping Jack.

"You mean a deserted one! There's nobody here, my dude!" Jack shouted.

"I have to admit, if somebody was here they would've shown themselves already," Otilia replied.

Frank took a deep breath and said, "Fine, you pick the lock, Jack. I'll go upstairs to see what's going on there. Otilia, stay with Jack." Frank said.

As Frank walked away, Jack asked Otilia, "What's wrong with your friend? We gotta be cool. Panicking will only make things worst. As a bounty hunter, I tend to do well staying cool. Such as picking this door, which is now open. After you, my lady,"

Otilia was impressed with Jack as she said, "You did good, sweetie,"

Jack was blushing after hearing those words. The two of them saw what they could gather from the armory.

Meanwhile, Frank checked to see what was upstairs. When he got to the detective's office, he saw Martha was killed by the rats as well. Her mouth was open as she appeared to be screaming before being torn apart. The bite marks were visible along with the pool of red blood. Frank cried when he saw the corpse of his friend. He had a crush on Martha when he was in high school.

Despite never going out with her, Frank and Martha were best of friends. While emotional, Frank knew he needed to stay strong. He looked around for any evidence. He checked the fax machine and saw a note.

In Spanish, the note read that the police were evacuating the population in the Mansiones de Salinas neighborhood. It was a rich neighborhood filled with mansions. It was also a gated neighborhood, which gave the police a defendable position. Frank now knew where to go next. It was clear that he needed to go east as the rats were probably not there yet.

As for what would happen when they got there, that was a different story. Before Frank could leave, he saw a group of rats in the back of the room. He screamed. Otilia and Jack heard the screaming.

"That's Frank!" Otilia shouted.

"Let's go save him!" Jack replied.

The two of them ran up the stairs. They followed the screaming, which led them to the detective's office. Jack and Otilia used their newly acquired weapons to take out the rats.

"Thank you!" Frank said, nearly out of breath.

"Look what we got!" Jack said while displaying the armor and weapons they got.

"I'm sorry for being pushy. As for me, I found out where we need to go. It's a bit of a drive, but I suspect once we get there, we might have a good chance of escape," Frank replied.

"What is it?" Otilia asked.

"This note points out an evacuation point. It's in a rich neighborhood. As I said, it's a bit of a drive. It's better than staying here, though," Frank answered.

"Alright boss, let's escape before those rats return. Also, I would grab some weapons and armor before you leave," Jack responded.

Frank nodded as he headed to the armory to grab what he could.

Jack, Frank, and Otilia now had a destination. Whether it would lead them to safety was another question. However, Jack was correct. Staying in their current location was not an option. The rats were closing in.

Chapter 7

Jack, Otilia, and Frank were still at the police station. They were looking around to make sure that the coast was clear. There was a small horde of rats coming from the front door. Otilia spotted the rodents.

The three of them shot at the rats, killing them all easily. Otilia was in shock that there were still many rats roaming around.

"Dios mio! How many rats are here? I could've sworn we killed an army of them!" Otilia said.

"My thoughts exactly," Frank replied.

"I got a feeling that this rat infestation has been festering for a long time, even before all this started. I reckon this might have started since those sugar farms were disturbed. This is just me saying this. For all I know, it can be all jargon," Jack told Frank and Otilia.

The trio figured that it would be near impossible to kill every single rat. Rodents were able to multiply much quicker than humans. Adding to that, these rats had glowing green eyes. That suggested that these rats were infected with a virus or were mutated.

The focus for the survivors was escaping to the extraction point. Once they got there, things would get a lot easier. It was just a matter of getting there safely.

"I know one thing is for sure. Staying here isn't going to solve anything," Jack told everyone.

"Agreed, let's get going while it's still early. The last thing we want is to be driving in the dark. Without power, these country roads will be too dark to drive through," Frank agreed with Jack.

Otilia didn't reply. She let the men make the decisions. With nothing else to do in the police station, the trio prepared to leave.

Frank walked to the pickup truck to start it. The truck looked to be untouched, which was an encouraging sign. He got in and turned the key. The truck didn't start. Frank's heart dropped, hoping that it was just in his mind. He turned the key again, but the vehicle wouldn't start.

"No! It can't be!" Frank said.

"What's the matter?" Otilia asked.

"What's the matter is that we're not going anywhere," Frank answered.

"Let me check this bad boy out. I'm pretty good with cars," Jack said, prepared to light a cigarette. Even during the worst of times, Jack needed a smoke.

He lit the cigarette as he opened the hood of the truck. Jack took a quick look at the hood and couldn't see anything obvious until he saw the suspect.

"Hey Frank, try to start the car again," Jack told Frank.

"Ok," Frank replied.

Frank turned the key. Once again, the truck wouldn't start. However, the car wasn't completely dead. It sounded like the truck wanted to start but couldn't.

"Well, I got good news and bad news. Which do you want first?" Jack asked.

"Does it matter? I assume no matter what, it means we're stuck here," Otilia answered.

"Ok... you're not wrong. The good news is that I know exactly what needs to be done. The bad news is that the battery is dead. Just chalk it up to just plain bad luck. The best case scenario is that we find somebody who can give us a boost or we find another car," Jack responded.

"Damn and to think we were getting our feet wet," Frank said.

"Can't we just walk to the evacuation point?" Otilia asked.

"It would take us many hours to reach there. Driving there isn't a big deal since we could speed there in about twenty minutes. If we have to walk, might as well kiss the idea of being rescued bye-bye. We won't even come close to getting there in time. Not to mention, those rats are bound to ambush us along the way," Frank answered.

"So you suggest we just stay here, do nothing, and let the rats eat us alive?" Otilia asked angrily.

"No... I was not suggesting that. Before you cut me off, I was about to say we should search for a new car. Or hopefully, we find a survivor that could give us a boost. Even if it means we have to take them with us," Frank answered calmly.

"Good idea, boss," Jack said.

The three of them started walking around the coastline of Salinas. The rain was still light, which helped the trio. Normally, this would be a perfect day to be by the water. On this day, the Caribbean Sea was choppy with high waves. The waves crashed onto the shore. They were so powerful, the water reached the trio.

Their feet were blasted with seawater. Jack worried if the waves picked up anymore, the seawater could flood the shore. He knew that seawater and cars didn't mix. The trio passed by cabanas that normally would be filled with clients. Instead, they were filled with carcasses of dead humans, probably the result of the rats.

"Who would've thought that rats would enjoy pina coladas by the shore? It's the stuff of nightmares," Jack told the others.

"Ha, ha. If that was your idea of a joke, it felt flat," Frank wasn't amused.

As the trio passed by the cabana's, some green eye rats helped themselves to some of the pina colada mixture inside a bar. It was the popular Ladi's place. It was renowned in Salinas for having some of the best pina coladas along with margaritas. It seemed that the rats were making themselves at home, much better than the humans were.

There was plenty of dead fish on the street as well. Some were swept by the waters, others were grabbed by the rodents. The trio arrived at the local beach in Salinas. Normally a bustling place with tourists, Polita's beach was more like a place where a meat wagon was needed. Dead fish and dead humans roamed the sand.

"What the hell is this? This looks like a graveyard, not a beach," Otilia said.

"You got that right," Frank replied.

"Is anyone around? We've come to rescue you!" Jack shouted, hoping for an answer.

As the three continued to walk through the beach, a rat was looking at them from one of the cabanas. Nobody had an idea they were being watched.

The rain started to pick up once more. It wasn't a downpour, but it was a steadier rain than before. Not even the beautiful coconut trees around the beach were enough to make the scene any less grim.

The three of them approached the most beautiful part of the beach. There was a tree that had grown on the beach. Rising sea levels submerged the root of the tree. However, it made for a nice spot for swimmers. The branches had grown over the seawater. Many tourists enjoyed staying in the water, under the tree. It provided them with much-needed shade during the warmer months. Not to mention, it made for the perfect Kodak moment. Or a Polaroid moment for those who liked having the positive picture instantly.

Otilia imagined her move to Puerto Rico would have many moments on the beach with her husband. However, he was gone, forever. Puerto Rico had turned into a survival horror nightmare. She started to cry.

"What's wrong?" Frank asked.

"My husband is gone. This was the spot we were supposed to be at today. We always wanted to share a kiss here since we first met. Without him, I don't see a point in staying here in Puerto Rico. Hell, I don't even think I'll be able to go back home," Otilia accepted the sober reality.

"If only we could find the source of these aggressive rats," Frank said.

"That's the million-dollar question," Jack gave his two cents on the situation.

The rat that was watching the trio squeaked loudly. It was so loud that the trio heard it. They had no idea where it was coming from. All of a sudden, there was a horde of rats that came out of the tree over the seawater. A few rats even came out of the water under the tree.

"Ambush!" Jack shouted.

"They can survive underwater?" Otilia asked.

The three of them could have shot the rats, but the horde was too large to do so. Instead, they ran from the rodents. As they ran, they fired some rounds, killing a few rats.

Everyone made sure to keep running and not slip. With any little slip, the hungry bastards could catch up to them. The squeaks continued to be heard.

"We can't keep running like this. There's gotta be a safe place!" Frank shouted.

Everyone kept an eye out for a place they could run to. There was a large abandoned building ahead. It might have been infested with rats, but it was easier to kill rats in a building than out in the elements.

"Head to the building!" Jack shouted as everyone followed him.

The building used to be a shoe factory that housed close to a hundred jobs. That was before the factory jobs started to be outsourced to Asia. Salinas was still a town with plenty of industry, but it was a dying business.

The trio saw the front door ahead. They rushed toward it and opened the door. Jack slipped and fell. That allowed some of the rats to catch up to him. A few of them got on him and bit him on the arm.

Jack's armor did its job of preventing the bites from getting too deep. However, one rat got Jack in the leg. The pain was excruciating, but Jack fought it as he kicked the rat off his leg. After getting free of the rats, Jack limped into the building. He and the others shot at the rats close by to prevent them from getting closer.

When Jack got into the building, Otilia and Frank closed the door. They locked the door with a steel bar to keep the door held in place.

Everyone took a moment to catch their breath. Frank took a peek and saw that the rats were retreating. He breathed a sigh of relief.

"That was too close," Frank said.

"Damn, that bastard got me!" Jack said in pain.

"Let me take a look," Otilia said.

The bite mark was pretty deep and blood was coming out. Otilia went around the building to see if there was anything to take care of the wound. She had some cloth from the supermarket to cover the wound for now. However, she needed to find some antibiotics to prevent the bite from becoming infected. With these rats, there was no telling if they carried any viruses.

"Listen, you stay here with Jack. I'll go and find something to cure that wound. We should be safe in here for now," Otilia said.

"I'm sorry that your first experience here on our island has to be such a horrific experience," Frank told Jack.

"Don't sweat it, man. I'm a bounty hunter. My job is dangerous by trade. I will say, I didn't think getting bitten by a rat was part of the job description," Jack said while chuckling.

"True, just hang in there. I think I might know somebody that could help us start the truck,"

"If so, it'll be a good idea to spit it out. We need to find a safe place. Going on the run will only get us so far. We need a place where we can draft a plan to get out of here," Jack told Frank.

"Ah yes, mi amigo, Clarke can help us. He's a gringo, from Washington State. However, he's very good with cars and is a prepper. I'm sure he's doing okay or at least better than us. He lives around here. When we get out of here, we'll head to his place," Frank told Jack.

Otilia had returned with some ointment she found. It was a bit dated, but it was better than nothing. She rubbed on Jack's wound. The sting was a bit much for Jack, but after a few minutes, he started to feel better. Otilia had him sit for a few minutes. She saw that the wound had gotten better.

"You think you can get back on your feet?" Otilia asked.

"I got to. We don't have any time to waste. Besides, Frank knows who can help us," Jack answered.

"Yep, let's get going. We don't have much time to waste!" Frank told everyone.

Jack was back on his feet. They knew the front door was not safe as the horde of rats would be waiting for them. Instead, they used the back door. It proved to be a good decision as there weren't any rats waiting for them.

Otilia and Jack followed Frank. Jack was able to put pressure on his leg. He still felt some pain, but it was something he needed to withstand. The three of them followed Frank through the beach town.

They approached a marina. Several large boats were behind the structure.

"We're getting close guys," Frank told everyone.

The rain picked up in intensity once more. After a couple of more minutes walking, they approached a white house that had an SUV and an RV. Also, there were large coconut trees in the backyard. A few mature banana trees were in the yard as well.

A large shack was by the trees. Jack was impressed and convinced that Clarke was a prepper. Before they entered the properly, they heard screaming from inside.

"That might be my friend. Come on everyone!" Frank shouted.

The three of them entered Clarke's property. The screaming was coming from inside. Frank saw that the door was open. He ordered them to follow him into the house.

When they entered the house, they saw what appeared to be a man in trouble. Rats were ready to attack him. He was armed with a bat with barbed wire. The man did a good job holding his own as he swung at the attacking rats.

However, the numbers game caught up to him. The rats started to gain the upper hand. Jack and the crew entered to help out the man. They didn't want to spread bulletholes on the man's house, so they didn't use their guns.

Instead, they entered with sticks and bats. The rats lounged at the man. The trio defended him as they swung at the rodents with their melee weapons. One of the rats got on the male, but he grabbed the rat and choked it to death. Green blood came out of the rat.

After a few minutes, the rat horde was defeated.

"Frank? What are you doing here? I mean thank you for saving me, but what do I owe this visit?" The male asked.

"Clarke, I came to check in on you. Thank goodness, you're still alive. I guess you met the rats as well," Frank said.

"Oh yes... We need to come up with a plan to get out of here," Clarke replied.

"We do have a plan. We have to go to the Mansiones de Salinas. We have a truck, but the battery is dead," Frank told him.

"Sit down, guys. You look like you need a drink of water or something," Clarke told everyone.

Everyone welcomed the bottle of water they were given.

Clarke was an American born in the Pacific Northwest. He was in his lower 40s. He was born in a rural area, so he knew how to live a minimalist life. Clarke was a huge prepper. At the same time, he was a man with a huge heart. Clarke was willing to help anyone who needed it, within reason at least. He loved the United States but experienced a nasty divorce. His daughter decided to live with him.

In search of a tranquil life, away from his ex-wife, Clarke decided to move to Puerto Rico. It was an island that was friendly toward ex-pats from the US mainland. Salinas was a spot where many ex-pats were moving to with the upstart neighborhoods being built. Not to mention, Camp Santiago was in Salinas. Camp Santiago was the biggest military installation in Puerto Rico, which attracted ex-pats to move to Salinas. Frank kept the camp in mind as an alternative destination in case the current destination proved futile.

Clarke had a sixteen-year-old daughter from his failed marriage. She had just gotten her driver's license. Clarke had two vehicles in his household.

"That feels better. Thanks, Clarke, but I need a major favor from you," Frank said.

"What is it, my friend?" Clarke asked.

"We need a boost for our truck. The battery died out. Can you give us a boost? In exchange, I'll let you follow me to the evacuation point that somehow the local government decided to hide from us."

"I would love to, but sadly my jumper cables were stolen. I know... I'm a prepper and my stuff gets stolen. Go ahead and make fun of me, hehe. However, I know a place in the Plaza de Mercado where we can get jumper cables. I can take you there, but I need a favor from you,"

"Fair enough. What do you need?" Frank asked.

"My daughter is stuck out there. The Plaza is ground zero for the rat infestation. It's too dangerous for her to get out on her own. The rats have that area on lockdown. Not even the police can break through. However, you guys look well-armed. We might stand a better chance of getting my daughter to safety. Will you help me?"

"Sure we will," Frank answered.

"Wait a minute, how did you talk with your daughter when the phone line is out?" Jack asked.

"I invested in satellite radios for our cars. They are still new but thank goodness I invested in them. She called me in a panic. I was heading there before the rats attacked me. Honestly, I would feel more secure if I could go there with you. If you save my daughter, I would be in your debt. Also, I would be happy to come with you to your destination. We gotta stick together," Clarke answered.

"It's settled then. Where is your vehicle?" Otilia asked.

"Over there by the palm trees. Hop on in!" Clarke pointed to his blue 1984 Ford Bronco SUV.

With that Otilia and the crew found themselves a new ally.

Chapter 8

Jack, Otilia, and Frank all jumped into Clarke's SUV. They rushed out of the house in case more rats were in the area. As they were driving, Jack gave Clarke a suggestion.

"Hey, I think we should stop off at the police station. It wouldn't hurt if you have more gear to take on the rats," Jack told Clarke.

"Hmm... I have a couple of handguns, but I could use some armor. Ok, let's go," Clarke agreed with Jack.

Clarke drove down the small beach road. They passed by the cabanas and small businesses as the rain picked up in intensity. The Caribbean Sea started to get choppier. The waves grew larger. Sea water started to spill onto the road.

"Crap! This is not good. The water is starting to get onto the road. As you may well know, salt water and cars don't mix well," Clarke told everyone.

"I'm aware. Our truck is near the police station. Hopefully, that's not too close to the water," Frank replied.

"The truck shouldn't get exposed to the seawater under normal high tide. Just pray that the waves don't get even worse.

"It's hard to see the beach so empty. I'm sure you guys get a lot of people here," Otilia said.

"Oh yes, this is a great tourist stop. Plenty of ex-pats such as myself chose Salinas to live in. Have you heard of Camp Santiago? It's the largest military base on the island," Clarke replied to Otilia.

"Did you serve?" She asked.

"No, I came to Puerto Rico after a nasty divorce with my ex-wife. I needed a place of tranquility. Frank was one of the first friends I made here. Thanks to him, I got used to life out here. I never thought we would be invaded by blood-sucking rats," Clarke answered.

"I'm sure nobody imagined that. There goes our truck up ahead," Jack told Clarke.

Clarke saw the truck and stopped his SUV in front of the police station. Everyone got out to make sure everything was clear. Clarke took a look at the Chevy C-10 truck. He wanted to make sure it was the battery and not something else.

Clarke had Frank turn the key. By the sound, Clarke determined that the battery didn't have enough juice to start up. Therefore, the battery was dead. Jack and the others were relieved to hear that.

"There might be a jumper cable in the police station," Frank thought.

"Hmm... good point. They're bound to have one. I think we should take another look," Clarke replied.

"Wait, how about your daughter?" Otilia asked.

"She's a strong girl. I'm sure she'll be ok until I get there. Besides, your friends make a good point of being prepared. We only have one shot to save her, so we better make it count," Clarke answered her.

The four of them entered the police station once more. Not much has changed besides the fact a police officer was lying on the ground. There was a pool of fresh blood next to the officer. There was green blood next to the body, suggesting that rats were responsible. With no phone service, everyone had to be careful.

Frank showed Clarke the armory. Everyone looked around for any survivors. There were none in the building. Clarke entered the armory, where he found the last remaining suit of body armor. He didn't need guns but did take a couple of handguns and magazines in case he ran out of ammo for his current weapons.

A horde of rats came from the outside. Clarke and Frank were on the first floor. Instead of running from the rodents, the two began firing at the hungry rats. Jack and Otilia heard the shooting and headed downstairs to help their friends.

Clarke showed off his shooting skills in front of everyone as he shot the rats before they could close in on him. A couple of rats sneaked into the police station and went after Otilia. Clarke spotted them and shot them easily. He blew on his gun after killing off the rodents. Everyone reloaded their weapons.

Jack went outside to make sure the coast was clear. Other than the rain, everything was quiet. No more rats were around.

"Nice shooting, Clarke," Frank said.

"Thanks... I got a lot of practice in the shooting range back in my hometown. I always knew the practice would come in handy," Clarke responded.

"Let's see if we find a jumper cable. I don't like that truck where it is. That seawater might reach it," Jack told everyone.

The four of them looked around the station but came up empty. Jack saw a door he didn't see before. He tried to open it but was locked. With his lockpick, Jack unlocked the door easily. He called everyone to where he was. Everyone rushed to his location in the back of the station.

"It's a maintenance room. We're bound to find something here," Jack said.

Everyone searched the large maintenance room. There were parts for everything ranging from lightbulbs to car parts for the police cruisers. There were at least 15 aisles in the room. The crew split up to search the large room. Jumper cables weren't hard to distinguish. It was the sheer size of the room that was intimidating. At least, the room was well-kept and clean. It even smelled like Pine-Sol, which was a welcomed scent. The floors were absent of any spills or dirt.

There were plenty of ventilation holes in the room, which kept the crew on alert. They spent a good ten minutes looking through the room. Frank found the car parts. He ordered everyone to search where he was.

After searching through the room, Frank found where the jumper cables should've been. There were no cables around.

"Damn, there's no cables here," Jack said.

"The police must have taken them in case anybody outside needs help," Frank replied.

"Too bad, I don't see any officers here," Otilia responded.

"We'll have to go to town and spot an officer. Maybe they can lend us a cable," Clarke said.

"Sure they'll give us a cable for a car that's down here. Get real, hermano, these cops are lazy! Besides, they won't waste their time coming down here. We have a better shot stealing a cable," Frank retorted.

"Ughh, good point. Well guys, we better get out of here," Clarke told everyone.

Before they could leave the room, the door to leave slammed shut. Squeaking could be heard coming from the ventilation shafts.

"Oh no, we gotta get out of here!" Otilia said in a panicked tone.

Rats started to come out of the shafts. They started to pack the maintenance room. Oitlia rushed to open the door, but it was locked. The door was a double deadbolt. Somehow the door was locked by someone, but who?

Without the key, the four were stuck inside.

"Jack! The door is locked!" She screamed.

Jack rushed to the door to try and pick the lock once again. Clarke, Frank, and Otilia had to fend for themselves until the door was unlocked. The three of them fired rounds at the rodents. For as many as they killed, more rats replaced them.

"How many of these bastards are there?" Clarke asked.

"They reproduce quicker than we can eradicate them!" Frank answered

"Come on Jack, we can't hold these rodents back forever!" Clarke shouted.

"I'm moving!" Jack shouted back.

Jack was fiddling with the lock. With the pressure around him, he had a tough time getting the deadbolt picked.

"Come on, come on!" Jack said, flustered.

The other three did the best they could to kill off the rats. However, the number of rats continued to grow at a quick rate. A few of them got close to Clarke as he was reloading. Frank stepped in the middle and smacked the rats with a metal pipe he found.

Two rats got on Frank and bit him on his left arm. Clarke reloaded his gun and fired at the rats who lounged at Frank. As for Frank, he grabbed the rats that had bitten him. The first one he choked while throwing the other one away from him.

Otilia reloaded her pistol as rats started to rush in her direction. The squeaking was enough to paralyze her with fear. She needed to stay strong, however. At the last minute, Jack got the door unlocked.

"Finally!" Jack said, relieved.

Clarke and Frank saw the door open. They rushed out of the room. Otilia was unaware that Jack had picked the lock. She braced for the rats to make her lunch. Jack saw Oitlia was in trouble and rushed to help her.

"Get over here!" Jack shouted as he pulled Otilila.

Otilia and Jack left the room. He wanted to close the rats in but didn't have the key to lock the door.

"We can't stay here! Those rats are on our tail!" Frank told everyone.

He wasn't lying. The rats were on their tail. They were hungry for human flesh. Everyone ran out of the police station as quickly as possible. The rats were hot on their tail. The squeaking was especially terrifying for Otilia, who feared rodents.

They eventually reached the front door. There was no time to embrace the beach scene.

"Quick, everybody inside!" Clarke shouted.

Everyone entered the SUV as the rats started to get out of the police station. Clarke started the vehicle and then floored it out of the area. The rats continued to chase the car. Clarke went as fast as possible but had to account for the small beach road. He didn't want to crash into anything.

The rain poured down on the car. Clarke turned on the windshield wipers, but they had a hard time keeping up with the heavy rain. Nonetheless, Clarke kept his focus on the road. Otilia looked behind and saw the rats still giving chase.

"What the hell are these rats!" Otilia shouted in fear.

"I have to agree these rats are persistent. I don't want to pressure you, Clarke, but is it possible to go a bit faster?" Jack asked.

"I'm trying! Unless we get out of the beach town, we're not going anywhere fast. These roads are too small to pick up much speed," Clarke explained.

"He's right. I was raised here and I know," Frank replied.

Clarke decided to speed up a bit, knowing the rats wouldn't stop chasing the vehicle. It was risky, but driving slowly was just as dangerous.

"Buckle up. It's gonna be a bumpy ride!" Clarke warned everyone.

Clarke drove faster as he made the hairpin turns. Everyone hanged on for dear life. The road was bumpy as well, making it an uncomfortable ride. Otilia was worried that Clarke would lose control or crash into a building. Jack did his best to calm her down.

Frank continued to look behind him. The rats were still chasing them. However, they were further from the vehicle.

"Good job! We're losing them. I'm sure when we get onto the main road. We'll lose them for sure," Frank said.

Clarke continued to drive over the speed limit as he made more heart-stopping turns. The rain continued to pour, making it tough for Clarke to see. He knew the road in the back of his head, which made it easier. There were only a few more turns to make before getting onto the main road.

Otilia was still panicked about the ride.

"We'll be ok, hun. I trust Clarke will lead us to safety," Jack told Otilia.

Clarke was driving at a decent speed. The water on the windshield caused him to nearly miss hitting the hardware store in front of him. He only had a second to react. So Clarke made a wild turn. The SUV got onto the sidewalk and nearly tipped over. Everyone screamed, bracing for the worst.

The SUV was able to get back on all four wheels. That was the last turn before getting to the main road. It was a straight drive to reach Route 181 to escape the beach. The rats made caught up, but Clarke floored it.

When he approached the intersection leading to the 181, he quickly turned right to head north. Once Clarke got onto Route 181, Otilia looked behind her. She saw that the killer rats were turning back.

"Whew! Gracias a Dios!" She took a deep breath while praising God.

"De veda! Ese tada muy peligroso. Puedeo dios estada viendonos." Frank said that God was watching them.

"I don't understand what you guys just said, but I must admit that was a wide ride," Jack followed.

"Alright guys, we're out of there. We're about five minutes from the center of Salinas. I hope you're ready to head into town. You can bet your ass it's going to be worst there," Clarke said.

"I'm sure it will be. That's where the epicenter of the infestation is," Frank replied.

"Otilia, you wanna stay behind?" Clarke asked.

"No, I'll be fine," Otilia answered.

"Besides, there's nowhere safe around here. I'm safer with you guys," Jack said.

"Ah, good point," Clarke replied.

Clarke drove until reaching the inspection leading to county road 3. He turned left as he was heading to town.

Jack was concerned about the seawater picking up. There was a chance that his truck would be covered in seawater. However, there was little he could do. He had to hope for the best.

Everyone survived their trip to the beach. It was the last place anyone considered dangerous. The main town was looking to be even worse.

It was only ten in the morning. However, time was ticking to reach the evacuation point.

Chapter 9

The crew was on country road 3, heading for the town center of Salinas. Clarke saw that gas wasn't an issue. However, what was an issue was that nobody had eaten anything. Hunger pains started to show.

The coffee shop might have had some good stuff remaining. Otilia and Frank were concerned about stopping there as it was probably infested with rats. With that in mind, they decided not to mention stopping there. The rain was still coming down, albeit not as heavy when the crew was on the beach.

As they were driving, a police cruiser swooped by them from the left. The cruiser had its sirens blaring. Based on the direction it was heading, the police car was heading to town.

There was little traffic on the road. Whatever cars were on the road were heading in the other direction toward the evacuation point. Otilia, Frank, and Jack wished they were heading there. They thought the nightmare would end if they could reach the evacuation point. Instead, they would be walking into the teeth of the rat infestation.

"I can't help but feel a bit nervous," Otilia said.

"Can't say I blame you," Frank replied.

"I think we'll be ok. We gotta keep the faith. After all, the only thing we got is each other," Jack said.

"I'm feeling a bit hungry," Clarke said.

"Maybe we should stop for a bite to eat," Otilia replied.

"Never mind, we have to rescue my daughter. She's a tough cookie, but even she has her limits. Also, I wouldn't feel right eating without her around. Unless you guys need to eat something," Clarke responded.

Everyone shook their heads. They knew the more time they wasted, the harder it would be to reach their final destination. As Otilia looked out her window, she saw what looked to be a giant rat. Before she could alert the others, it was no longer there. She wanted to say something, but without proof it was there, it would be a waste of time to mention it. Otilia figured it was just a product of her imagination.

She didn't want to stress out the crew, as there was already enough to worry about. Another police cruiser went around them at a high speed.

"What's with these police cruisers?" Jack asked.

"Whatever is happening in the town is probably huge," Frank said in fear.

"We gotta hurry! My daughter might be in serious trouble," Clarke responded.

Clarke saw the road blocked by a police barricade. There were plenty of police officers guarding the town center. Police vehicles and equipment were taking up all the parking on the main road.

As he pulled up on the barricade, Clarke lowered his window to talk with the officer.

"You can't be here. It's too dangerous for anyone to be here. The rats have this place under their control. You need to turn back now," An officer told Clarke.

"My daughter is in the Plaza de Mercado! I gotta save her," Clarke told the officer.

"Our men are in the town, rescuing those they can reach. I'll be sure to let my men know there is a girl at the market. You have to go. We can't risk any more civilians dying on us," the officer replied calmly.

"I need to rescue her. It's not that I don't trust you guys. I'm just worried. Let me in there!" Clarke started to become aggressive.

"Sir, you need to calm down. If you don't turn around, I will be forced to arrest you and your friends for obstruction," the officer wasn't amused by Clarke's attitude.

"My daughter is in there! Don't you understand English?" Clarke insisted.

"Are you going to turn around or do I put the cuffs on?" The officer asked.

While Clarke was worried about his daughter, he knew getting arrested wouldn't help his cause. To save her, he needed to be free.

"Please, Clarke, just listen to the officer. I'm sure the police are doing their best," Otilia tried to instill some sense into Clarke.

Clarke thought about it for a minute.

"Ok, officer. I'll turn around. But if anything happens to my daughter, I'm holding you and the force responsible," Clarke told the officer.

"Now that's better. If anything, wait for us by the gas station. If we find your daughter, we'll be sure to bring her there. Keep the faith, amigo. Now go on,"

Clarke reluctantly turned around. He didn't have much faith that the officers would rescue his daughter.

"Are we really going to turn around?" Jack asked.

"What choice do we have? We're asking for trouble if we try to barrel through the barricade. Trust me. We won't get far," Frank answered.

"I'm sure the officers will get your daughter," Otilia tried to calm everyone down.

"So we'll gonna trust what a bunch of men in uniforms say? Because I sure don't," Jack retorted.

"You seem to be a rebel, heh?" Frank asked.

"I'm a bounty hunter, after all. I catch criminals the police can't. Let's just say, I don't think very highly of police officers. Don't get me wrong. I appreciate what they're supposed to do. It's just that I think plenty of them don't take their job seriously enough or abuse their rank," Jack answered.

"I have to agree with Jack. There are a few good men in the police force here. However, many of them don't pull their weight. Now if we can bump into my friend, Robert that would be great. Robert is a friend of mine that I grew up with. He moved to NYC to be an officer there since the pay was better. Just like me, Robert got tired of living where he was. So he chased a life in Puerto Rico. Robert works in the police force here. He's a really good guy. I'm sure he would help us more," Clarke told everyone.

"What are you suggesting?" Otilia asked, worried that Clarke was planning something stupid.

"There's no way I'm standing around at a gas station to wait for my daughter to be brought to me. Besides, I saw those officers. They don't seem to be in a hurry to rescue anyone. If anything, they are just standing there to look important and collect their paycheck," Clarke replied.

"Wait a minute, so we're going into town?" Frank was confused.

"Yes, we are. Now I'm not stupid enough to drive through the barricade. Instead, we're going to sneak into town through the back streets. They might have the front side of the town closed up, but I'm willing to bet that the back side is soft as jelly. Normally, I hate to break the law. This is my daughter, however. I'm willing to do anything to save her," Clarke answered.

Nobody challenged Clarke at that point. They agreed that standing around wasn't a good idea. It would kill valuable time they need to reach the evacuation point. Clarke knew there was a back road he could have taken.

He turned back to the officer's satisfaction. He reached the fork in the road by the gas station. There was a road that led to the back roads of the main town. Clarke made a U-Turn to get onto the side street.

The rain started to lighten up a bit. Clarke drove slowly as he turned right on a one-way street. The street was surprisingly empty, with only a few cars parked. More importantly, there were no police cruisers around. As he drove by a road leading to the center of town, he saw another police barricade. It wouldn't be smart to park on that street.

He continued driving slowly. There was a pharmacy ahead, but it was boarded up and tagged with police tape. There wasn't anything else around the area other than some abandoned buildings and a store that sold farming equipment.

Clarke saw a good area to park. It was close enough to the Plaza de Mercado but far enough to avoid police attention.

"This is as close as we'll get. It's not much of a walk to the Plaza de Mercado," Frank told everyone.

"We'll have to be sneaky. I'm sure they're police officers patrolling the area," Clarke said.

"I reckon we can be quiet," Jack told everyone.

Otilia said nothing. She just wanted to get out of there. The four of them got out of the SUV, ready to explore the market.

They started walking down the side road that led them to the market. As they closed in on the market, they saw two police officers standing guard.

"We'll have to get around them," Clarke said.

"I know, we can go around these homes," Frank replied.

They were technically trespassing but figured nobody was around. Everyone jumped over the gate into the property. A cop was patrolling the street. Everyone hid behind the garbage can to avoid being detected. The cop looked around for anything.

Jack peeked from his location to see what the cop was doing. When the cop walked away, he gave the thumbs up to continue.

Everyone went around the wooden house. It was occupied, so they had to be careful not to attract any attention. When they reached the backyard, the crew saw a middle-aged female on the floor. Against their better judgment, the crew tried to get a response from her.

Otilia saw there was a deep puncture wound on the woman's neck. The woman had no pulse either.

"She's dead. However, it looks like she wasn't torn apart... eww..." Otilia freaked out when she saw green blood coming out of her.

"What's happening to her skin?" Jack asked.

The woman's skin was furry. It was almost non-human. The crew had no idea that the rats would use certain bodies as hosts. They feared that the woman was transforming. Those fears were put to bed when Oitlia couldn't find a pulse on the woman.

Jack saw the door leading inside was locked. He pulled out his lockpick to pick the lock.

"What are you doing? That's someone's house!" Frank whispered loudly.

"The homeowner is dead bro, chill. Besides, we have to see if there's anything we can use," Jack replied.

"I don't advocate breaking into people's homes, but the person appears dead. What might be inside will prove more useful to us than her. I also recall that you guys need a jumper cable to get your truck started. There might be one in here. It's at least worth exploring," Clarke said.

"Ok, as long as we don't get caught," Frank replied.

Jack got the door picked. Everyone quietly entered the house, making sure nobody saw them. When they entered the house, the crew saw it was vacant.

Everyone started to investigate the house for anything useful. Otilia kept her eyes on the window, looking at the guarding police officers. Gunshots were heard close by. Everybody got on the floor to avoid getting hit by stray bullets.

"Oh fuck, the rats must be here. That sounds like the police are shooting at the rats," Jack said.

The town sounded like it was in the middle of a warzone. Otilia saw the officers guarding the street rush towards the front of the Plaza de Mercado. Gunshots continued to ring off. Some sounded closer than others. This was the last thing Otilia expected when she moved to Puerto Rico.

No one had any idea if the officers were winning the battle or not. However, they had their money on the rats. When the gunshots calmed down, everyone got up from the floor. There was a lone rat inside the house, eyeing the crew.

The rat came from under a sofa and lunged at Jack. It got onto his neck and bit it.

"Oh fuck! This little bastard got my neck!" Jack shouted in pain.

Jack was taken to the ground as the rat bit on his neck. Otilia grabbed the rat from Jack's neck and removed it. The green-eyed rat started into Otilia's eyes. She was instilled with fear when she saw the rodent. The rat was ready to bite her as well.

Otilia panicked and threw it onto the concrete wall. While the impact injured the rat, it continued to move. The rat lounged at Clarke, ready to attack him. Clarke kept his cool and sidestepped. He avoided the rat from getting onto him. When the rodent struck the floor, Frank grabbed his stick. With it, he struck the rat repeatedly until it perished.

Green blood gushed out of the rat. Some of it went on Frank's clothes. He quickly tried to wash it off.

Jack was in severe pain. His stomach was killing him.

"Oh man, that rat must've been venomous. My stomach is killing me," Jack said in pain.

"You might be poisoned. Let me see if there's anything I can make to get rid of the toxins," Otilia said.

Screaming was heard coming from the market.

"That's my daughter!" Clarke shouted.

"We can't leave Jack here. He's in serious pain," Frank retorted.

"My daughter is in trouble. If you want to stay here, be my guest. I'm going to help my baby!" Clarke replied.

"Clarke, at least take Frank with you for support. I'll stay here with Jack to nurse him back to health," Otilia calmly said.

"I can help Clarke out. Let's get going," Frank said.

Clarke nodded his head. He and Frank left the house to go to the market.

Otilia placed Jack on the sofa for him to lie down. She looked around for anything to help him. To her luck, the homeowner had some packets of green tea. She got busy boiling the tea.

While she waited, Otilia went to comfort Jack.

"Oh man, this stomach pain isn't making things any easier," Jack said.

"Let me see your neck," Otilia replied.

When she checked the neck, she saw that the bite had gone in deep into his neck. She wasted no time finding something to cure the wound. Otilia found some hydrogen peroxide, perfect for curing cuts and wounds.

"This is gonna sting, but be a big boy," Otilia warned him.

She applied the peroxide to Jack's neck. He screamed a bit due to the sting. A few minutes passed and the sting wasn't as bad.

"Only a couple of minutes until the tea is ready,"

"Thank you, Otilia. You're pretty badass,"

"Why, thank you. I just happen to be good at nursing people back to health."

"I think you're more than badass. Honestly... I think... any man would be lucky... to have you," Jack said in pain.

"My husband was lucky to have me. However, he's gone. I still miss him, though," Otilia said.

When the tea was finished, she poured a cup and gave it to Jack. He started to drink the tea. While it was hot, Jack felt it going down well in his stomach.

"How do you feel?" She asked.

"I'm feeling better, thank you," he answered.

"Just keep drinking and you'll feel better. Frank and Clarke went into the market to save Clarke's daughter. Don't worry. You stay here with me getting better,"

"I'm sorry about your husband, by the way," Jack said.

"Thanks, at least he's in a better place. He doesn't have to suffer here with me,"

"If it makes you feel any better, my girlfriend passed away last year due to cancer. It's been a miserable year being solo. It's why I became a bounty hunter. At one point in my life, there was little to live for,"

"I'm so sorry, Jack. You have something to live for, even if it's just to save yourself and us. I'm sure once you get out of here, things will improve,"

"Once I escape this crazy island, everything else will seem easier. I'll say that much,"

"How's the tea?"

"It's really good. You really outdid yourself. My stomach is starting to get better. I wasn't kidding when I said any man would be lucky to have you,"

"Aww, you're a sweetheart. It's a bit too early for me to be thinking about someone else,"

"I understand. You just lost your husband. What will you do once you survive?"

"I don't know. It's too early to think about that. I have a feeling that this survival adventure isn't going to end anytime soon,"

"Sadly, I agree with you. Who knows if it's just here? I doubt it's just here in Salinas. I'm sure the rats must be moving through the island,"

"Yet with all that, I feel hope. I believe we'll survive all this,"

Otilia held Jack's hands and said, "As long as we stick together, we can overcome anything. I'm glad that we met," Otilia said emotionally.

"Aww... you already have given me more confidence since this all started. I hope that our friendship goes beyond just this adventure. However, if our friendship is only meant to last until this adventure, I won't fault you,"

Jack held his mouth closed as he wanted to puke.

"Are you ok?" She asked.

Jack got up and headed for the bathroom. He vomited his guts out. It was green mucus and other toxic crap. It appeared that the green tea killed the venom before it could settle in his body.

It was a painful puke for Jack. However, he felt a lot better after vomiting. Jack took a few minutes to recover before returning to the living room.

Before he could get comfortable, more gunshots rang out. He and Otilia got back on the floor until the shots stopped.

"I hope Clarke and Frank are going to be ok," Jack said.

"I'm sure they will. Just rest here. They are getting Clarke's daughter and be right back,"

"I hope so, but something tells me we might have to go and help them,"

"I sure hope not,"

Otilia and Jack sat on the sofa, waiting for the return of Clarke and Frank. The rain picked up in intensity. The officers were fighting off the rat hordes the best they could. Jack seemed to have feelings for Otilia but decided to keep them to himself.

Chapter 10

Otilia and Jack continued talking among themselves. Jack was starting to develop feelings for Otilia. He knew that it was too soon to do so. After all, she had lost her husband just a few hours ago. He feared that she would be just a memory once this survival adventure was over. On the other hand, he wanted to respect her feelings and not seem desperate.

He wondered how Clarke and Frank were doing.

***

Frank and Clarke jumped the gate and ended up back on the street. There was no fear of being caught by a cop. All the cops were engaged elsewhere. More gunshots rang out. The two of them hid behind a car to avoid being shot.

As they left the safety of the car, they heard a male shouting.

"Freeze!" A cope ordered the two.

"Shit, we're busted," Frank said.

The two of them turned around to face the officer. Clarke recognized the officer.

"Robert?" He asked.

Robert was Clarke's friend. He was a childhood friend of Robert. Robert moved to NYC after getting a job offer that was too much to pass. He was in his mid-forties. Unlike Clarke, Robert was a no-nonsense man.

He had to be in his job. Robert was considered one of the top officers in the Salinas police force. Criminals feared him. Also, many of the young kids disliked him due to his strictness. However, Robert always made sure his friends were taken care of.

"Clarke, what are you doing here? Get back home now! I don't want to arrest you," Robert ordered the two.

"Listen, Robert, just for one second, please," Clarke answered.

"Ok, Clarke," Robert replied.

"My daughter is stuck inside the market. I need to save her. I know you guys have this area closed off. My friends are armed and ready to defend themselves. I ask you to let us go and save my daughter. Or even better, why don't you come and assist us,"

"Normally, I wouldn't entertain that. However, you and I are childhood friends. I hope I don't regret this, but I'll give you guys a hand," Robert agreed to help.

"Excellent, we now stand a better chance," Frank said.

"We need to be careful. The market is a pretty big building. That means lots of hiding places for the rats," Robert warned the men.

The three of them walked carefully through the streets of the town. The rats were loose. So they could have been anywhere. When they turned the corner, a small horde of rats popped out from a trash can. They wasted no time shooting the rats before they could get any closer.

Otilia saw Frank and Jack escorted by Robert. She had no idea that the officer was friendly. She rushed out of the house to try and help her friends.

"Hey, get away from my friend or I will shoot!" Otilia shouted.

Frank, Robert, and Clarke turned around and saw Otilia aiming her pistol at Robert.

"Whoa! Put your gun down! This is Robert. He's on our side. I can promise you he is," Clarke told Otilia.

Otilia put her gun down. She felt better that Robert was an ally.

"I feel better. Jack is feeling better," she told the guys.

"Good, just keep an eye on him. We can take care of ourselves," Frank told Otilia.

"Ok, que dios te proteja," she told the men.

"You have more friends, Clarke? Also, did you break into that house?" Robert asked.

"Sort of. The front door was open. We heard screaming and tried to save the homeowner. Sadly, she was eaten alive by the time we got in," Clarke told a small fib.

"I see. I'm glad to see you tried to save your fellow residents. Now I don't have to get you for breaking and entering, hehe," Robert joked.

Clarke and Frank laughed along. The three of them continued to walk around the market. There were two ways in, but the back entrance was locked. As they got to the front of the market, more rats appeared in front of them.

The three of them shot the rats. As they walked forward, they started to smell tear gas.

"Tear gas!" Robert shouted.

"We gotta get out of here. That stuff will kill ya," Clarke said.

The tear gas was used to try and slow down the rats. However, the rats seemed not to mind the tear gas. They enjoyed the toxic gas. However, the officers couldn't have anticipated that.

The three of them waited for the gas to dissipate before moving further. What was normally a bustling market was nothing more than just a graveyard. There were plenty of dead bodies. It was a combination of civilians and cops lying on the ground.

The rain picked up in intensity once again. It was safe to say that the weatherman was dead wrong about the forecast.

Frank, Robert, and Clarke made it to the front of the market. From there, Clarke could hear his daughter screaming. When they reached the front of the market, they saw that the metal door was padlocked.

"What the hell? Why is the door locked?" Clarke asked angrily.

"I don't know... I wasn't here when that was done. I was in the town square. If I had to guess, it was to keep the rats from having any more hiding spots. Sadly, it seems your daughter has been locked inside. I was under the impression the market was still open," Robert answered.

"It sounds like you had no idea. What do we do now?" Frank asked.

"The lock has chains. If we can cut the lock, we'll be able to break in," Clarke answered.

"Ah, we have bolt cutters inside one of our emergency vehicles. Sadly, we have to get to the town square. It's not too far from here. There's a heavy concentration of rats there, however," Robert said.

"That doesn't scare me. I'll do anything to save my daughter. Also, there might be other survivors inside," Clarke replied.

"We don't have time to waste. Those rats are bound to find a way in the market," Frank told the men.

"Right, let's get going!" Robert said as he had the men follow him.

"Don't worry, baby, I'll be back to get you," Clarke said.

The three of them walked straight down the street as it would lead them to the town center. There were a couple of pharmacies, food vendors, liquor shops, and clothing stores. Most of the stores were boarded up.

They continued walking and saw the town square was only a block away. However, more rats continued to pop out of nowhere. The three of them teamed up to shoot the rodents. A couple of rats got by as they lounged at Robert.

The rodents bit him on the arm. Clarke and Frank grabbed both rodents and shot them on sight. Robert favored his left arm as he dropped to his knees.

A couple of rats saw Robert down and attempted to bite him. Clarke saw the rodents and dropped to the floor. He slid in front of Robert as he shot the killer rats.

"Are you ok?" Frank asked Robert.

"I'll live. It'll take more than a bite to keep me down," Robert answered.

Robert and Clarke got off the pavement. When everybody was up, they started to walk to the town square. As they walked, green blood was splattered on the buildings and pavement. It was a disturbing sight.

Frank could only imagine what the people of Salinas did to deserve such a fate. He was a religious man. Frank believed that the power of faith would help him. With what was happening, he found himself questioning his faith.

"Why would God allow such a disaster to hit my town of Salinas? I still have faith. Perhaps it's to clear the population of all the sinners. However, I don't think Ruben was a sinner. I don't know. For now, I need to survive. I'm sure my questions will be answered then," Frank said, in his head.

Frank caught up to Clarke and Robert. As they walked, Robert continued to favor his left arm. Despite the heavy rain falling, they finally reached the town square.

There were a few cops around. They were fighting against a horde of rats.

"We gotta help my brothers in blue. Follow me!" Robert shouted.

Clarke and Frank kept up with Robert. The cops were by county road 3, in front of the mayor's house. Rats were overwhelming them. That was with even tear gas being shot at the rodents. The gas did little to slow down the rats.

Robert, Frank, and Clarke started to fire at the rodents, helping to even the odds. The police officers appreciated the help, even if it was from outsiders. When the horde of rats was defeated, the officers cheered. The scene turned peaceful.

Even the rain stopped. The clouds above started to open up and the sun peeked through. Everyone felt, despite the massacre, the terror was over. They had won the war.

"Thank you, guys. I admit, we wouldn't have defeated them without you. I'll be sure to get the mayor to give you the keys to the city," the police sergeant told the men.

"That won't be necessary. All I need is to borrow a couple of bolt cutters to cut the lock at the market. My daughter is stuck in the market. Also, I hear screaming coming from inside," Clarke told the sergeant.

"Ah, yes. We locked the market to keep the people safe from these rats. With the coast being clear, I can get the door opened for you," the sergeant said with a smile.

"Thank you," Clarke replied.

"Alright men, keep your eyes out for any more hordes. I believe it's a bit too early to celebrate,"

Frank and the others believed that the sergeant was correct. It was a bit too easy. At least, the sun tried to peak out after all the rain that fell. It was a moment of solace for everyone.

The crew followed the sergeant to the van. Inside the van, there were a pair of bolt cutters. Clarke was relieved that he would rescue his daughter. When the bolt cutters were obtained, the skies darkened once again.

"Welp. at least the sun came out for a few minutes," Robert said.

With the bolt cutters in hand, the crew headed back to the market. Some squeaking was heard in the distance. Nobody was surprised to hear rats were around. However, nobody had any idea where the rats were.

"I hear rats, come on guys, we better hurry," the sergeant said.

The men rushed toward the Plaza de Mercado. When they looked to the right, they saw a giant rat. It was much bigger than the others. The rat was about the same size as the height of a small business, which was about ten feet tall.

"Lord have mercy! What the fuck is that?" Frank asked.

"It's trouble and we better get moving!" Clarke answered.

The men had no idea what to do. They could either take on the giant rat or run. They decided to try to fight the giant rat. Clarke, Frank, and Robert started to empty their bullets at the rat.

The giant rodent rushed toward Clarke, trying to tackle him. He dived from the attack. He continued to fire his gun at the rodent. The rodent squeak loudly.

Green blood came out of the rat's mouth. With its tail, it whipped all four men down to the ground. The giant rat walked up to the sergeant. The police sergeant tried to fire his weapon, but it was empty. He needed to reload.

The rat tore the man apart limb from limb as it ate the police sergeant whole. Frank and the others were in disbelief at what they saw.

"Holy shit!" Frank shouted.

Robert remembered there were some grenades in the emergency van.

"Hey, keep the rat distracted. I got something that can defeat that big pest," Robert shouted at Frank and Clarke.

Frank and Clarke kept the rat distracted as Robert obtained grenades from the van. He grabbed a couple and rushed back to the battle. When he reached the rat, he threw the grenade at the rodent.

"Grenade!" Robert shouted.

The bomb exploded on the rat, causing it to burst into pieces. The blast also caused one of the nearby buildings to sustain serious damage. Blood and rat parts were splattered on the town center.

When the giant rat was killed, the men wasted no time returning to the market. They didn't want to chance any more rats chasing them. Upon reaching the market, Clarke took the bolt cutters and cut the lock.

With the lock broken, the men quickly entered the market. There were plenty of dead bodies on the ground already. When Clarke reached the last storefront on the right side, he had found his daughter.

"Papa!" Clarke's daughter shouted as she went to hug his daughter.

"Oh man, am I glad to see you," Clarke said, nearly crying.

It was a heartwarming scene in the middle of a dangerous survival horror adventure. For a moment, the men could enjoy a small victory.

Chapter 11

Clarke embraced his daughter. He thought she wouldn't be around when he got to her. It was a heartwarming moment in what was otherwise a dark situation.

She was 16 going on 17 and an honor student in school. While she was young, she was a brave girl. Clarke raised her to be a prepper just like him.

"I'm glad you came for me, papa. It was so horrible. We were hiding in here, but the rats got in here. I don't know how I survived," Clarke's daughter told her father.

"The rats got in here?" Robert asked.

"Yes... I just defeated the rats with wits. Sadly, a couple of market workers didn't. The rats tore them apart limb from limb. I just want to get out of here," Clarke's daughter cried.

"These rats are smarter than I thought," Robert replied feeling concerned.

The crew saw the dead bodies of the market workers. Clarke's daughter was not lying about the carnage around her. Clarke knew it was time to leave before the rats could enter.

"I'm proud of you, baby. You are a strong girl. I feel you will be a strong woman when you get older. Thanks guys for helping me," Clarke said.

"I'm glad to have helped you. We have to stick together at this point," Frank replied.

"A promise is a promise. I'll give your truck a boost when we get to the beach, if we find jumper cables," Clarke told everyone.

"Hey Robert, you want to tag along with us?" Frank asked.

"I guess it wouldn't be a bad idea to jump along, now that my superior is dead. Besides, I'll probably have to find a new job once this is all done," Robert answered.

The crew looked around the market. It was the center of commerce for Salinas. There were various shops. They were mostly food vendors. The food sold ranged from fried pork rinds and pork sausages to empanadas. Mostly traditional Puerto Rican food was sold, which was rather tasty.

The market was a great place to come and mingle with the locals on a hot day. The aluminum roof helped keep the sun from beaming down. Also, it was a great place to relax and listen to fine traditional music on a rainy day. This was the place to be in Salinas besides the beach. Since Salinas was still growing and technology still hadn't caught up, this was the place many residents spent their free time. Cable television was still considered a luxury that hadn't reached Salinas in the mid-80s.

However, looking around, the market was completely dead and deprived of any noise or people for that matter. The beautiful murals on the walls were desecrated with green blood from the dead rats. Human blood was mixed in as well.

There was an auto parts store to their left. The door was wide open. Without anyone looking after the store, the crew entered. They found a set of jumper cables in the back of the shop. Clarke saw the cashier was torn apart by the rats. He heard squeaking but couldn't find any rats.

"I'm hungry," Clarke's daughter said.

"Girl, I think there's bigger things to worry about than your stomach," Frank replied.

"Hey now, she's valid to feel hungry. Not to mention, it's not a good idea for us to keep going without eating anything," Clarke retorted.

"I guess you're right," Frank said as his stomach made a loud noise.

"How about we grab a bite to eat from one of these shops," Robert told everyone.

"I don't necessarily trust the food here. We'll end up eating leftovers from yesterday since they haven't had the chance to cook fresh food today," Frank said.

"Yeah, that's true. Getting food poisoning isn't a wise idea at this point. We're better off getting a sandwich from the gas station. At least, they'll be cool and fresh," Clarke agreed with Frank.

"I wanted a pull pork sandwich," Clarke's daughter whined.

"Same here, baby, but we might not be able to go home. We can't afford to get sick. As preppers, we got to be smart and not let our emotions get the best of us," Clarke reminded her daughter.

"I guess you're right," she replied to her father.

"Let's catch up with Jack and Otilia," Frank told everyone.

Everyone agreed with the idea. Before walking out of the market, the sound of squeaking was heard again.

"Oh, come on, not more of these guys!" Frank whined.

"No rest for the weary, I guess," Robert replied.

A horde of killer rats was outside, searching for their next meal.

"There's too many of them to fight out here. Let's head to the restaurant, we stand a better chance of picking them off!" Clarke told everyone.

The crew rushed through the wooden doors into the restaurant. It was a beach-themed restaurant with bamboo tables and chairs. Their specialty was cold pina-coladas, which were popular with the people. It rivaled those served by the beachfront. They also served traditional Puerto Rican food, which included rice with pigeon peas, roast chicken, and smoked pig.

This beautiful restaurant was now the scene of the last stand for the crew. When they got into the establishment, they hid behind the bar area. As the rats entered, Frank, Robert, and Clarke started shooting at the rodents. Clarke's daughter simply kneeled next to her father as instructed.

"Don't stop shooting or it's your ass!" Robert told the men.

Some of the rats made it through the barrage of gunfire. A few of them even made it to the bar area. Clarke's daughter saw the rodents. She knew she needed to do something. She grabbed a couple of beer bottles. One of the rats lounged at her father.

"Papa, watch out!" She shouted.

She pushed her father and bashed the beer bottle at the rat. The impact killed the rat instantly.

"Are you out of your mind? Get back down!" Clarke shouted at his daughter.

"But..."

"But nothing! I don't want you to get hurt,"

The men continued to defend themselves against the large horde. Clarke's daughter couldn't bare to see her father struggling. However, the men seemed to have a handle on the situation.

There was one more rat that was unaccounted for. It made a b line towards Clarke. His daughter saw that her father was unprepared for the rodent. She feared that it would bite him on the neck.

Against her father's wishes, she rushed to her father. When she got to him, she pushed him to the floor. The rat missed Clarke and landed on the floor. Frank struck the rat with his stick and impaled it. Green blood came out of the rat when it died.

"Why did you push me?" Clarke asked.

"I'm sorry, papa, but that rat was getting close to you. It almost bit you," she answered.

"She's not lying. Look at the bastard here. I killed it. A second later and you might have been torn apart," Frank replied.

"Wow, thank you, baby. I'm sorry I got mad at you. I just didn't want anything to happen to you. I guess you also want to protect me as well," Clarke told his daughter.

"You have a good daughter there. By the way, what's your name, young lady?" Robert asked.

"Jessica, but I prefer to be called Jessie," she answered.

"You're a brave girl indeed. I wish I could say things are going to get better. However, I truly believe they won't. These rats are multiplying faster than we can kill them. This was always a danger I worried about when they started building over their habitat," Frank responded.

"You might be right but there's nothing we can do about that now. It's about surviving and escaping, right papa?" Jessie asked.

"Yes, baby," Clarke answered.

The crew got up from the wooden floor and started investigating the restaurant. They were curious if there were any more survivors.

Everyone followed Robert into the kitchen. When they entered, it was quiet. All of the stoves were off. Nobody was in the area. It was clear, with no evidence of the rats entering.

"The coast is clear. It looks like the rats haven't reached here," Robert said.

What was normally a busy kitchen prepping for lunch was eerily quiet. There was no movement other than the crew themselves. A loud bang was heard to the right. Everybody expected to see more rats.

However, it was nothing more than a fallen pan. Relief was felt on the crew members' faces. The search for any more survivors turned out empty.

"Well, there are no survivors here. I think it's time for us to get going," Robert said.

"Agreed, the more we stay here, the more danger we put ourselves in," Franks replied.

There was squeaking heard through the ventilation shafts. Panic set in on the crew. There was no time to react as rats were popping through the shafts. The kitchen quickly grew crowded with the rats infesting it.

The crew was outnumbered. More rats came through another ventilation shaft.

"Oh, my god! More rats!" Jessie shouted.

"Quickly, to the exit!" Robert shouted.

As the crew ran out, Jessie slipped and fell to the floor. Everyone turned around to see Jessie on the floor. The rats closed in on the poor girl, ready to tear her apart.

"Papa!" She screamed.

Before Clarke rushed to his daughter, Robert beat him to the punch.

"You want her. You'll have to get through me first!" Robert stepped in front of Jessie.

The rats were hungry. Instead of going after Jessie, they jumped on Robert. He was overwhelmed by the rodents, as he fell on his back. Jessie got up and ran to her father.

"Robert! No!" Clarke shouted as he saw his best friend being eaten alive.

"I can't believe it... They're eating him like he was a piece of pork. My god!" Jessie turned pale.

"Forget about him. We gotta get out of here before they make us their next meal! Come on!" Frank shouted.

It was painful to see Robert dying. Clarke knew that his best friend sacrificed himself to save his daughter. He felt terrible that there was no way for him to return the favor.

Everyone rushed out of the market, leaving Robert to be torn apart by the rodents. Clarke couldn't get the sight out of his mind. The rain continued to fall at a decent clip. Frank and Clarke rushed to close the door to prevent the rats from following them. They chained up the metal door with the padlock.

That would buy them some time. The crew headed back to the house to meet Otilia and Jack.

"Everyone, we don't have time to relax. We gotta get out of here. Those rats are after us!" Frank shouted.

"Crap!" Jack replied.

Everyone got out of the wooden house. They rushed to Clarke's SUV. Everybody got inside. Clarke turned the key, hoping nothing happened to the vehicle. When he turned the key, it turned on to his relief.

"Buckle up everyone!" Clarke told everyone.

He floored the SUV and escaped from the town center. The rats had taken over the town center. All of the remaining police officers were torn apart. Their bodies lay defeated on the ground for the rats to feed on.

Clarke drove around the side streets until getting back on county road 3. When he got to the main road, things turned a bit peaceful. There was a bit of time for everyone to get to know Jessie.

"Everyone, meet my daughter, Jessie," Clarke said.

"Howdy partner," Jack replied.

"Hey Jack, you look like a cool guy," Jessie told Jack.

"Aww, thank you," Jack replied.

"Hi, Jessie, I'm Otilia. I just moved here," Otilia told Jessie.

"I'm sorry that your first day in Puerto Rico has been so bad. I promise you that the island is peaceful," Jessie told Otilia.

"I'm sure it is, but I'm happy you're safe," Otilia responded.

"My daughter is hungry. I honestly think that it would be wise to stop off at the gas station for a bite to eat," Clarke told everyone.

"I'm starting to agree," Frank said.

"Gas station food, yippie," Jack cheered.

"You seem to enjoy the gas station," Jessie told Jack.

"In my line of work, I have to. I'm on the road quite a bit,"

"What do you do, Jack?" Jessie asked.

"Normally, I would keep that secret, but under these circumstances, it doesn't matter. I'm a bounty hunter," Jack answered.

"Cool," Jessie replied.

"I guess it's cool, hehe," Jack said.

The small talk continued as Clarke continued driving to the gas station. He checked his SUV and saw it needed gas. There was a gas tank in the back that could be used to fill Jack's truck.

Rain continued to fall as Clarke drove down the road. Traffic had dwindled significantly. Not even police cruisers were driving by. Everyone was concerned that they might have been the only survivors in the area.

Otilia's original plan of calling the police was down the drain. Only the National Guard was left. Chances though, the National

Guard was at the evacuation point. The time on Clarke's SUV indicated it was near one in the afternoon. That didn't leave the crew much time to reach the evacuation point.

They figured getting to the area would prove challenging. At the moment, hunger plagued everyone. Five minutes later, Clarke reached the gas station. As suspected, it was empty.

"Oh no, are we too late?" Otilia asked.

"I hope not," Frank answered.

Clarke and everyone got out of the vehicle, ready to explore the gas station. To their relief, the gas station was still open. However, there was no power.

"No, we're too late. Without power, how are we going to pump gas," Jack said.

"Good point..." Clarke said, defeated.

"How much gas do you have?" Otilia asked.

"I have enough to get to the Mansiones de Salinas. After that, it's going to get tricky," Clarke answered.

Jessie walked around the gas station to see if there was anything around. To her surprise, there was a gas tanker in the back of the gas station.

"Hey, I found a gas tanker," she shouted.

Everyone followed her to see what she was talking about. She was telling the truth.

"What a good find!" Clarke said happily.

"How is that a good find?" Frank asked.

"We can pump the gas straight from the tanker. There's no power in the station, but we don't need power to pump gas from the truck... Don't you see, we don't need power to pump gas," Jack explained.

"Yes, I get it. Let's pump the gas then," Otilia said.

"Right," Clarke replied.

Clarke drove slowly to the tanker. The gas tank on the SUV was on the right side, so he parked close to the tanker, with the right side next to the tanker. From there, he and Jack got the hose. They placed the hose into the gas tank of the SUV.

Clarke saw the keys were still in the tanker. He turned on the truck. When the truck started, he and Jack pumped gasoline into the car until the tank was full. When that was done, Clarke got the five-gallon tank from the back of his truck. He filled it to the top. That would be to fill Jack's truck when they got it started.

When the two men finished with the gas, Otilia had a question.

"Wait, why don't we just travel with your car?" Otilia asked.

"I wouldn't mind, but it would be smarter to travel with two vehicles. In case one car craps out, we still have the other to use," Clarke answered.

"Ah, that's smart," Frank replied.

"I'm getting hungry," Jessie complained.

"I have to agree with the young girl," Jack said.

"Well, let's head inside," Clarke replied.

"Alright, let's see what they got," Otilia said.

The crew checked around the gas station. Jack headed for the sandwich section. There were plenty of premade sandwiches in the fridge. He grabbed a turkey and cheese sandwich. Despite the power being out, the sandwich felt cold still. That was an encouraging sign.

Next, he grabbed a beer out of the fridge. Everyone grabbed a sandwich and drink of their choice. It wasn't ideal, but they could ill afford to be picky. Jack took a bite of his sandwich. As quickly as he bit into it, he spat out the food into the trash.

"Ugh, it's spoiled. I hate that!" Jack whined.

"Spoiled, you sure?" Clarke asked.

Everyone except Jessie ended up spitting out their bites in disgust. Jessie ended up enjoying her sandwich.

"Mmm... tasty," Jessie said.

"Count on her to be the lucky one not to get a nasty sandwich," Frank replied.

"Try your beer," Clarke told Jack.

Jack tried his beer and ended up spitting it out as well.

"Man, that's the worst beer I've tried. It's flatter than an old tire," Jack told everyone.

Not taking any chances, everyone grabbed a bottle of water and some snacks. That turned out to be a better choice.

"At least the water and snacks are good," Frank said, looking at the bright side.

Clarke spotted a radio on the counter where the cashier would be normally. He turned on the radio to hear the news.

The radio station in Salinas was out of order. Frank changed the station to hear the radio station from San Juan.

When they heard the news, the reporter was reporting news from parts of Puerto Rico. He noticed that Salinas was never mentioned. The reporter had shunned Salinas and ignored what was happening. It was as if Salinas did not exist, which angered Frank.

"Why am I not surprised!" Frank said.

"What do you mean?" Otilia asked.

"The government of Puerto Rico always ignores Salinas and the towns close to us. It's as if we don't fucking exist!" Frank answered.

"That is strange. Why would they not report it? Could it be they don't know?" Clarke tried to be reasonable.

"Oh, come on, Clarke! You're giving the government here too much credit. They hate us here. To them, we're nothing but a bunch of hicks and uneducated delinquents," Frank kept talking down on the island.

Clarke slapped Frank and said, "Whoa! Calm down, man! I know you're angry, but this is not the time to get political," Clarke scolded Frank.

"Why? Because you still want your daughter to believe in fairytales? Get real, dude! The spoiled sandwiches and beer here are the perfect metaphor for how the suits up there see us. To them we don't exist and if we perish, so what. We're nothing but dead weight to them!" Frank continued.

"No, I refuse to believe that," Clarke replied.

"Let me ask you this. Do you see the National Guard here? Do you see a huge response here? Do you see any emergency vehicles coming here? No! The only thing we have is an arbitrary point on a map. A point nobody was going to tell us. We only found it in a police station. And who knows if that evacuation point is legit? They might have left us in the dust already! So no, Clarke, I believe that we've been left for dead for these rats to finish us off!" Frank went on a rant.

"Clarke, it might just be that Frank is right, even if he sounds like a total buffoon when explaining," Jack told Clarke.

"If so, we only have each other to rely on," Clarke accepted that Frank was probably right.

"So we're going to die here?" Jessie asked before crying.

"No honey, we're going to survive," Otilia comforted Jessie before looking at Frank angrily.

"Listen, you can look at me angrily all you want. I'm just telling you the truth. I'm sorry that it hurts," Frank shouted.

Jack grabbed Frank and placed him in a headlock.

"I'm getting sick and tired of your rants. Do I have to put you to sleep?" Jack asked.

"Jack, stop!" Otilia shouted.

"Jack, calm down. We need to stick together if we're gonna survive. Fighting with each other isn't going to help. I admit that Frank might have said it in the wrong way, but I think he might be correct. So let him go," Clarke told Jack.

"Really, you believe this lunatic?" Jack asked before letting Frank go.

"I'm a lunatic because I tell the truth. Who grabbed me and threatened me? Heh?" Frank asked.

"Stop it, you two. Clarke is right. We need to remain cool. We all want to survive. The way I see it, we have to take care of ourselves. I don't think we're getting any help from anyone else. Are you two going to calm down?" Otilia told everyone.

"Ok, I'll be cool," Jack said.

"Same here," Frank replied.

"We don't have time to waste. Let's get back to the beach so we can give your truck a jump start," Clarke said.

Frank and Jack made up. The next destination was the beach. Time was ticking, though.

Chapter 12

The crew accepted the reality of being solo in this survival horror adventure. Frank might have been correct that the government of Puerto Rico left Salinas for dead. He hoped he was wrong. The rain continued to fall at a decent clip.

Clarke looked around the gas station. As much as he didn't agree with Frank, he realized he might have been right.

"Who would've known that we would be left here to die," Otilia said.

"You see all this spoiled food around us. That's what the rest of Puerto Rico sees us as. We're nothing but a spoiled and rotting town on an otherwise beautiful island. This is poetic justice gone the wrong way. Now you see what your 'brothers and sisters' think of you. Salinas is a blue-collared town, but the suits in San Juan want to ditch that proud identity we have. The truth hurts, but all you need to do is look around you," Frank ranted.

Clarke wanted to retort but couldn't. After all, Frank wasn't wrong. Everyone was stuck in a gas station filled with inedible food. There was no help around or on its way. They were truly alone in the middle of a killer rat infestation.

"All we can do now is head back to the beach and get my truck started," Jack said.

"And hope that the seawater hasn't risen too much," Clarke replied,

Everyone jumped into the SUV as time was running out for the crew to reach the evacuation point. When Clarke started the SUV, he was relieved to see he had a full tank of gas. At the same time, his confidence dipped. This was not normal for a prepper like Clarke.

He had spent his life preparing for the apocalypse. While for the most part he had done well, Clarke still felt lost in this situation. It was still hard for him to believe that the main branch of Puerto Rico was oblivious to what was happening in his town. He was concerned that perhaps Frank was right. There was also the possibility that the government was purposely letting Salinas sink. After all, it would be one less town that the governor of Puerto Rico would have to support.

The possibilities were in Clarke's head. He needed to get that out of his head. It was about surviving at this point.

As the SUV pulled out of the gas station, a rat came out of the gas station staring at the vehicle. It squeaked, causing other rats to join the rodent.

Clarke drove from the gas station back onto Route 181, heading south. Everyone was a bit nervous to head back to the beach. They remembered there was a large horde of rats that chased them out. However, a second vehicle would drastically increase their chances of survival.

Unlike their first trip to the beach, the crew found it was no longer the beautiful gem it used to be. It looked like a hurricane had hit the area. There were more dead bodies on the ground. There were plenty of tire tracks at the entrance to the neighborhood, suggesting that people were trying to escape from the rats. As Clarke continued to drive through the small streets, he noticed some of them filled with seawater.

"Shit!" Clarke said.

"What's wrong, papa?" Jessie asked.

"The seawater is flooding in. I hope it's not too high or you can forget about your truck, Jack," Clarke answered.

The waves coming from the sea were huge and crashing onto the shore. Seawater from the storm surge was getting onto the streets of the beach. While minor flooding was normal for the area during storms, the surge of water was higher than normal.

Time was of the essence. Clarke needed to get to the truck before the water got too high. The most direct route to the police station was cut off due to the flooding, making it too dangerous to drive through.

"What's wrong?" Otilia asked.

"The water is too high. Clarke could try to drive through, but there's no need to take a chance. The last thing we need to happen is for the car to die in the water," Frank answered.

Clarke turned around from the flooded street. He had to maneuver around the smaller roads. It took him longer to get to where he needed to be. At least, the streets were still relatively dry. A few minutes later, the crew reached the truck.

To their relief, the truck was still dry. However, the seawater was creeping closer to the truck. There was no time to waste.

"Good, the truck is still dry," Jack said.

"Perhaps, but the storm surge is the highest I've seen in ages. We need to hurry before the water gets too high. If that happens, there's no way we're getting out of here," Frank replied.

The seawater was rising at a quick pace. Combined with the heavy rain falling, the crew needed to get the truck started fast.

Clarke parked his SUV in front of Jack's truck. He opened the hood of the SUV. Jack went to open the hood of his truck. Otilia grew nervous about the rising waters.

"Hurry up! The water is creeping up!" Otilia shouted.

"Damn, she's right. That water is creeping up fast. This is unusual for April," Frank replied.

Rising seawater and sea storms were ultra-rare in April. This backed up Frank's theory that Salinas was a forsaken town. He rushed to help Clarke. Frank grabbed the jumper cable from the back of Clarke's SUV.

"Here you go," Frank handed Clarke the cable.

"Thanks," Clarke replied.

Clarke carefully connected his side of the cable on the batter of this SUV. When he was done, it was Jack's turn to connect the other side of the cable to his truck's battery.

"This better work!" Jack told Clarke.

Clarke didn't reply as he entered his vehicle. He started the truck and revved up the gas. Jack then turned on his truck. However, the engine wouldn't start when he turned the key.

"It's not turning on!" Jack shouted.

"Keep trying!" Clarke replied.

Clarke kept revving up the gas to charge Jack's truck battery quicker. Once again, Jack turned the key on the truck. The truck still refused to start. Panic started to dwell in for everyone. The seawater started to close in on the vehicle.

"Oh man, this is cutting it close!" Clarke said, grinding his teeth.

"Come on, come on!" Jack shouted.

Despite five failed tries, Jack and Clarke didn't give up. The water was on the tire of Jack's truck. Clarke continued to rev the engine on his SUV, hoping it would be enough to boost Jack's truck.

"Ay dios mio, la agua!" Otilia screamed about the rising water.

The water was starting to over a quarter of the tires of both vehicles. Time was running out.

Clarke's desperation paid dividends as Jack's truck finally started.

"Yes! Quickly, get the cables out. We have to get going!" Clarke told Jack.

While Jack and Clarke removed the jumper cable, the seawater was overtaking the beach. Cabanas by the shore drowned under the seawater. The main beach road was buried under feet of water. The beach bars were submerged in seawater. It would take quite an effort to rebuild what was buried under the seawater.

"Jack, meet me by route 181!" Clarke shouted.

Jack nodded in agreement.

What was supposed to be a beautiful beach day was a total disaster. Otilia, Jessie, and Frank saw the disaster in front of them. Clarke ordered his daughter to get into the SUV with him. Jack, Frank, and Otilia all went into the pickup truck. Clarke drove right out of the police station.

Meanwhile, Frank had to do a tricky U-turn to escape. The water was nearly overtaking the tires on the truck.

"Hurry up before this truck begins to float!" Jack shouted.

"I'm trying. This is not an easy turn!" Frank retorted.

After some effort, Frank drove out of the police station. He was on the main gastronomy road. Otilia looked at the right-side mirror. She saw the seawater flowing into the police station. The flood water had overtaken the area. It was a sad sight to see.

Frank continued driving until he reached Route 181. When he got there, he saw Clarke's SUV parked there. He got next to the SUV and had Otilia open her window.

"I'm happy you got out of there," Clarke told Frank.

"Ok, now onto the evacuation point," Frank replied.

Looking at the time on the truck, it was already four in the afternoon. Time was flying by. They couldn't afford any more issues or detours. The way to the Mansiones de Salinas was a straight drive down county road 3 East. Both Clarke and Frank knew how to get there, so they didn't have to worry about following each other. Nonetheless, if they stood together, it allowed a higher chance of survival.

The rain stopped once they left the beach area. When both cars reached the light at the intersection, they turned right on county road 3. They drove past the gas station with the spoiled food. Traffic was non-existent. It was quiet, with no movement.

As they drove through the farmland of Salinas, no horses or cows were around either. The crew believed the rats might have eaten the animals.

The drive was rather peaceful to start. Frank passed the local high school, which meant they were halfway to the evacuation point. Everyone was feeling more confident that this nightmare was about to end. The sun tried to peek out from the clouds.

They hoped it would come out completely. Any sunlight would lighten the mood, even by a trivial amount. The power plant was nearby, which represented three-quarters of the trip. The time was closing in on five in the afternoon. That only left an hour to get to safety. The day had flown by.

The last thing they wanted to do was be stuck in the streets of Salinas when the sun went down. That was especially true without any light or phone service. However, everything seemed to have turned for the better. Frank was shocked when he saw a large truck driving behind them. He was encouraged, figuring the driver was heading to the same place they were heading.

As the truck drove closer, Frank and Clarke realized it was out of control. The truck was going full speed ahead, ready to crash into them.

"What is wrong with this guy? He's about to crash into us!" Jack shouted as he pulled the steering wheel to the right. That forced the truck to veer to the right onto the grass.

Frank realized the truck would strike him if Jack didn't grab the wheel. Clarke was ahead of them. Frank banged on the horn, hoping Clarke would hear it.

Clarke was driving in peace until he heard the horn. Jessie saw the truck in the rearview mirror.

"Papa, go right! That truck isn't going to stop!" Jessie shouted in panic.

Clarke saw the truck and drove to the right as the truck drove by at full speed.

"What the hell is wrong with that guy?" Clarke asked.

Nobody knew the driver was eaten by rats that were in the truck. He did the best he could to fight them off. The numbers were too much. A couple of rats got to his neck and ripped the flesh off it. The driver was dead.

There was nobody to stop the large vehicle as it went full speed. The truck started to drift to the right until it struck a huge power pole to the right of the road. The impact was so severe, the transformer on the pole exploded. The metal on the bottom portion of the pole bent.

A few minutes later, the power pole fell onto the road, blocking it. Clarke and everyone else were in shock.

"Holy moly! As if this adventure couldn't get any crazier," Jack said.

"I hope we can get around that pole or we're screwed," Frank replied.

Meanwhile, in the other vehicle, Clarke checked that his daughter was ok.

"Are you ok, Jessie?" Clarke asked.

"I bumped my head, but I should be ok, papa," she answered.

"I'm sorry... Well, if you look at that?" Clarke replied.

"Big trouble, that's a power pole," Jessie responded.

"Correct and it's blocking our way," Clarke said.

Clarke and Frank both drove close to the pole. When they closed in, they saw the electrical pole covering the entire road. Before they came up with a plan, they saw the rats pop out of the truck.

"Jessie, get behind me!" Clarke shouted.

Jessie got behind her father. The other four started to shoot at the killer rodents. The horde wasn't all that big, so they killed the rats easily.

"Lookout!" Jessie shouted as she spotted a small horde of rats trying to ambush the party from behind.

Jack rushed in front of everyone. He shot the rats with his machine gun.

"That was close. Thanks, kiddo," Jack told Jessie.

"Yeah, good one kid. However, what are we going to do about getting through here? This is the only direct road to the Mansiones de Salinas," Frank asked.

"Wait a minute, you can't be serious," Otilia retorted.

"Sadly, I'm not. This is the only road that heads there. It's just our luck that this pole fell. And yes, it's too heavy for us to lift," Frank replied.

Clarke walked over to the driver. When he reached the driver's seat, Clarke wished he hadn't. The driver's neck was torn apart. Blood was pouring out of his neck. He couldn't bare to see anymore.

"This wouldn't have happened if that driver wasn't driving like a maniac!" Frank shouted.

"Whoa, brother! I've been around plenty of truck drivers. They would never drive like that unless something happened to them," Jack retorted.

"Like what?" Frank asked.

"Follow me to the truck. You'll see," Clarke told everyone.

Everyone walked to the truck and was greeted with the grueling scene of the dead truck driver.

"Oh my god! Those rats even break into trucks?" Frank was shocked.

"Sadly so, these rats are intrusive little bastards," Clarke answered.

"So what do we do now?" Otilia asked.

"Good question," Jack answered.

"I don't know. Honestly, we're running out of time. If anyone has any bright ideas, it's time to come up with them now," Frank answered.

Everyone looked at each other for answers. The only thing they could have done was drive around the pole. However, there was a ditch to the left of the road. There wasn't much space for a car to fit through.

There were too many trees to the right, which blocked cars from going through. Clarke, the prepper, was stumped on this one.

"Are we really stuck here?" Jessie asked.

"No, honey. I'm sure we'll find a way out of here," Otilia said as she hugged Jessie.

Otilia was trying to be positive but knew the situation was dire. The only positive thing was the rain had stopped.

Chapter 13

The crew looked at the downed power line in doom. There was no way they could lift the pole, even with the effort of everyone. The rain had stopped falling.

Everyone was encouraged when it looked like the skies wanted to clear. However, they knew this game well. Just when the sun was beginning to come out, the dark clouds covered it.

"So what are we going to do now?" Frank asked.

"I was thinking maybe walking to the evacuation point, but that would prove risky," Jack replied.

"Not to mention, it's still a long walk to get to the Mansiones de Salinas. We won't get there in time," Clarke added.

"Even if we can't get there in time, we stand a better chance of survival with our vehicles over going on foot," Jack mentioned.

There was still the idea of getting around the power pole safely with the vehicles. Clarke saw just enough room for both vehicles to get through safely.

"I have an idea, but it's risky," Clarke told everyone.

"I'll take a risky idea over just standing here, feeling sorry for ourselves," Jack replied.

"We drive our vehicles to the left of the road. There is just enough room to get through without falling into the ditch," Clarke explained his idea.

"Whoa, whoa! You expect me to drive through that little area?" Frank asked angrily.

"It's either that or we're stuck here," Otilia replied.

"Listen, you can stay here and feel sorry for yourself. I for one, refuse to do so!" Jack retorted.

"Yeah, when you fall in the ditch, come back to me," Frank responded.

Jack was boiling mad. He wanted to punch Frank in his smug face.

"Dude, you might be the most negative person I've met. Since I've met you, nothing but negativity has come out of your mouth. If you weren't my teammate, I would totally knock you out," Jack vented.

"The truth hurts. I'm sorry that it stings. However, as I said, we've been left here for dead," Frank replied.

"That's such a loser's attitude, bro. There's no reason to make it political. I don't know politics here and quite honestly, I don't give a flying fuck about your government. Making this political isn't helping. If you want to survive, you've got to put in the effort and not cower out. Or maybe you want to be eaten by a rat. I might not know the government here, but I do know Puerto Ricans," Jack retorted.

"So you do, huh? Looking for a gold star? I'm surprised that there are Ricans in Tennessee," Frank got smart with Jack.

While Jack wanted to slap Frank, Otilia did the honors instead.

"Shut the fuck up! Even I'm sick and tired of your bickering. How about being a 'real' Puerto Rican and growing some balls!" Otilia ranted.

"Yeah, my best friend back in Gallatin is Puerto Rican. He's a hardworking dude. Even when things get tough and boy has he had it bad, he stays strong. Let's just say I'm confident that he's been through more than you have," Jack told Frank.

"What do you know of my life, gringo?"

"My 'gringo' redneck face knows that you need to get it together and fast. It's not going to get any easier. I suspect you've had an easy life. You look like the kind of person who runs from the first bit of adversity," Jack told Frank to his face.

Frank turned his back and walked away from everyone.

"Frank, where are you going?" Otilia asked.

"Let him go. He's just doing what he normally does. Walking away with his tail tucked between his legs," Jack taunted Frank.

"Que pendejo! What did you say?" Frank shouted.

Frank turned around and was tempted to punch Jack in the mouth.

"You won't do shit to me," Jack said confidently.

Frank balled up his right hand into a fist. Everyone anticipated a fight. Then Frank put his hand down in defeat.

"Ready to be a man and stop looking at the negatives of everything?" Jack asked calmly.

"I guess so. Not that I have a choice," Frank answered.

"If it makes you feel better, I'll drive the truck," Jack replied.

"No... I want to prove myself. I'll drive," Frank retorted.

"Alright, that's more like it," Jack said, encouraged by Frank's attitude shift.

The truth was, the crew only had each other to rely on. After the verbal dispute, the survivors were ready to drive both trucks through the small clearance.

There was just enough room, but the driver had to be careful not to make any sudden shifts to the left into the ditch. Also, driving too far to the right would cause the pole to cut into the truck.

Clarke decided he would go first to drive his vehicle. He carefully lined up the SUV with the space in front of him. Otilia would guide him on his left while Jessie watched the right side.

The skies were still bright despite being cloudy. Without rain, Clarke had an easier time watching what was in front of him. When he was ready, Clarke took a deep breath as he drove slowly forward.

The ladies were guiding Clarke as best they could. Clarke continued to drive slowly through the hole. The left wheel of the SUV was barely on even land. The ditch was right next to it.

Frank and Jack watched nervously as Clarke had to remain focused. The right of the truck was barely missing the metal on the fallen pole. It was literally threading the needle.

"Come on papa, just a little more," Jessie said in her head.

After two minutes of carefully driving, Clarke made it through the hole. He drove back onto the main road, feeling relieved.

"You did it, papa," Jessie said as she rushed to hug her father.

"Well, it's your turn, brother," Jack told Frank.

Frank swallowed before getting into the truck. As he was getting in, there was a rat in the ditch watching everyone. Nobody knew if the rat was there or if it was solo.

"You got this, man," Jack told Frank.

"Thanks... Sorry for getting all crazy on you," Frank replied.

"It's all good," Jack responded.

Frank took a deep breath as he entered the vehicle. He didn't need to but wanted to prove to Jack that he was a team player. More importantly, he wanted to prove to himself that he wasn't weak. He started the engine on the truck.

Frank carefully lined up the vehicle with the hole. He took another deep breath before starting to drive forward. Just as they did before, Otilia and Jessie guided Frank.

Frank took his time getting to the open lane. The left tires on the truck were dangerously close to the ditch. Out of nowhere, Frank heard squeaking. When he heard that, he got cold feet. He stopped driving forward.

Everybody wondered why he had stopped. He opened his window.

"Why did you stop? I'll guide you. I promise not to lead you the wrong way," Otilia asked.

"It's not that. I heard a noise," Frank answered.

"I don't hear anything," Jack replied.

"You sure? I could've sworn I heard rats," Frank asked.

The squeaking was heard again. This time, it wasn't just Frank who was hearing it. Clarke and the women heard the squeaking.

"Wait a minute. Frank isn't lying. I hear something as well," Clarke said.

"Hmm... I don't hear anything. But I reckon if y'all are hearing something, it must be true," Jack told everyone.

There was squeaking, but no one knew where it was coming from. When it became clear that nothing was around, Frank started to head back to the truck. Before getting into the truck, he slipped on a wet rock. Frank rolled into the ditch.

"Are you ok, Frank?" Otilia asked.

"Yeah man, my arm is bruised, but I'll live," Frank answered.

Frank did what he could to climb out of the ditch. It was too deep for him to get up. The ditch was used to control flooding on the road during hurricane season and large rainstorms. Salinas didn't have a proper sewer system yet, so ditches and canals were plentiful. It was yet another result of Salinas falling behind in infrastructure.

In his mind, Frank thought that if he was in San Juan, he wouldn't be worrying about ditches. However, he continued trying to climb out of the hole with no success. When it became clear there was no way out, the others thought of a way out.

"Clarke, you're our resident prepper. Don't you have a rope to get our friend out of there?" Jack asked.

"I do. I'm getting it now!" Clarke replied.

He rushed to get the rope from the back of his SUV. Jack told Frank to relax and wait for the rope to be brought down.

As Frank waited for the rope, a horde of rats was behind him. He turned around to see the horror that was staring at him.

"You gotta be kidding me! There's more of these bastards?" Frank asked.

Jack and the others looked at the rats as they closed in on their prey.

"I can't stand here and watch this. I gotta help Frank out!" Jack said.

Jack went down the ditch to help out Frank.

"What are you doing here? Looking for a death wish?" Frank asked.

"Perhaps so, but if I kick the bucket, it'll be worth it. There was no way I was going to let you fight these rodents on your own," Jack answered.

Frank realized this was the real value of friendship. In his upper 30s, Frank saw he still had a lot to learn in life. At the moment, survival was the name of the game.

Jack was armed with his machine gun, while Frank had his pistol. They both started to shoot at the rats. Otilia would help out when she could by shooting rats within her range.

At first, the rats went down easily as Jack emptied his machine gun into the horde. However, he was out of ammo for his machine gun.

"Damn! What a bad time to run out of bullets," Jack told Frank.

"I'm low on ammo as well!" Frank replied.

They defeated the first horde of rats, but more of them continued to pop out.

"How are these guys outnumbering us? I'm sure we must have killed hundreds of them already!" Jack asked.

"Rats can breed and multiply quicker than us. I must say, though. These don't look like ordinary rats," Frank answered.

"No shit, Sherlock!" Jack retorted.

"I'm just saying these little bastards must be infused with a virus or something. These aren't ordinary rats... Look out!"

Frank saw a rat heading for Jack. He swung his stick at the rodent before it could reach Jack. Clarke got the rope and lowered it to Jack and Frank.

"What is Jack doing down there?" Clarke asked in a panic.

"Rats ambushed Frank down there. Jack wanted to help him," Jessie answered.

Ignoring his daughter, Clarke told the men to grab onto the rope.

There were too many rats to kill. Without guns, Jack and Frank knew that running was the only way out. Several rats tried to lounge at the men. They were able to defeat the rats with their sticks. For as many as they killed, they were more rats popping out from the depths of the ditch.

"We can't beat them all. Grab the rope!" Jack told Frank.

"Ok!" Frank replied.

Both men grabbed the rope. Clarke and the women held onto the rope to avoid it from falling.

"Hang on, ladies! Whatever you do, don't let go!" Clarke told the women.

As Jack and Frank climbed up the rope, a rat managed to jump onto Frank's leg and bite it. It was a painful bite, but Frank had to hold the urge to scream. He needed to get to safety first. Fighting through the pain, Frank climbed the rope and made it to safety.

Clarke pulled the rat off Frank and threw it back into the ditch. Frank was in too much pain to drive. So Jack decided to take the keys to the truck and drive.

"Get out of the way, ladies. I don't want those rats to get close to y'all!" Jack told Otilia and Jessie.

He got into the truck and drove through the lane. The adrenaline in his blood prevented him from worrying about driving into the ditch. It was about escaping from the rats. Within a minute, he drove the truck onto the county road. Frank was still in pain. Otilia still had some cloth left and tied it on the wound. The rain started to come down, once again.

"Thanks, I'll be alright," Frank told Otilia.

When both trucks were on the road, Jack saw there was a giant rat beyond the ditch.

"Guys, we better rush out of here. Look over there. It's a fuckin giant rat!" Jack shouted.

"Crap, we can't defeat that beast. We need to get going," Otilia replied, trying to hold her terror in.

Frank fought through his injuries to get to the truck. He decided it was wise to let Jack drive. Everyone rushed to their respective vehicles. Clarke and Jack floored their vehicles to get out of there. Jessie looked behind her and saw the rats were a safe distance from everyone.

"Whew, that was close," Jessie told her father.

"Yes, it was. There goes my rope, but at least it came in handy for something," Clarke replied.

In Jack's truck, Otilia was relieved that everyone was ok.

"Did we lose those bastards?" Frank asked.

"I think we're safe for now," Otilia answered.

"What time is it?" Jack asked.

Frank saw the time and answered, "It's five-thirty. Assuming there are no more roadblocks, we should make it to the evacuation with just enough time to spare," Frank asked.

"How far are we?" Otilia asked.

"We're about five minutes away from the neighborhood. Let's hope they didn't decide to leave early," Frank answered.

"Good, I'm just about ready to get out of here," Jack replied with a sigh of relief.

"Hopefully when we get there, they will lead us to safety. There is only one other place we can go to, which is Camp Santiago," Frank said.

"Where is that?" Jack asked.

"It's north of here. The only way to access it is through the town center or route 181,"

"Wait a minute, didn't you say this was the main artery that allows us to go east to west?" Otilia asked.

"Precisely. With the power pole in the way, it's going to be a bitch to get back to Route 181 if we need to do so. Hopefully, we won't have to take that route," Frank answered.

In Clarke's vehicle, his daughter asked him a question.

"Papa, do you think we'll be out of here when we get to the evacuation point?"

"I hope so, Jessie," Clarke answered somberly.

"Why do you hope?" She asked.

"I know I try to be a positive person. At the same time, I have to be honest. I don't know what to expect next. The drive was supposed to be smooth. Lots of things out of the ordinary have happened to us. When it comes to survival, I always said that you need to prepare for the worst. It's ok to hope for the best, but this is not a normal situation. I wish I could give you a better answer, honey. I wish I could," Clarke answered.

"It's ok, papa. I want you to know that I love you," Jessie said as she held her father's right hand.

"I love you too, Jessie. Stay strong, ok? We'll make it through this hell, one way or another," Clarke kissed his daughter on the head. He hoped this wasn't the last time he would kiss his daughter.

Everybody was hopeful that when they got to the evacuation point, it would mean the end of this nightmare. However, the drive to the Mansiones de Salinas proved to be hellish. It was hard to discount the idea that this adventure was far from over. One could hope, though.

Chapter 14

Clarke and Jack were driving down county road 3. The rain started to pick up again.

"So much for sunny skies," Otilia ranted.

"We have bigger issues than the weather," Frank replied.

"Pay attention. Let me know if I'm getting closer," Jack told Frank.

"Don't worry, there's a sign you can't miss," Frank responded.

The time on the truck read five-forty in the afternoon. That would give the crew just enough time to reach the evacuation point before everyone left.

Everyone felt hopeful that getting to the evacuation point would end their adventure of terror. Anxiety took over everyone's mind. They had gone nearly the entire day not seeing a large group of people. They were getting used to the idea of living life without a sense of normalcy.

"You were good, Jack," Otilia told him.

"Aww, you too, sweetie," Jack replied.

"I'm just glad this is about to be over," Otilia said.

"Same here," Jack responded.

"I don't think this is over. I'm sorry to say. You guys are totally wrong," Frank said somberly.

"Come on, bro, don't be so down. I know shit has happened, but you must believe. We can't be that unlucky. Now put that frown upside down," Jack told Frank.

"I'll try," Frank replied with a small smile.

"That's the spirit! We should be there soon," Jack said happily.

Despite the heavy rain, everyone was anxious to reach the Mansiones de Salinas. The road was completely deserted, which was a bit alarming. Everyone figured there would be some last-minute traffic heading to the evacuation point. However, they had the road all to themselves.

The sun was starting to set, which was concerning. Without working traffic lights, it proved dangerous to drive on the county road. It would prove even more treacherous if they had to take the rural roads.

Luckily for the crew, they found no traffic or any more detours to knock them off course. After an uneventful five-minute drive, the crew reached the Mansiones de Salinas.

Los Mansiones de Salinas was the exclusive neighborhood of Salinas. It hosted the elites of the town. Most of the neighborhood was filled with a few mansions that spanned much of the land. At the same time, it kind of symbolized the inequality of Salinas. Most of the town was either lower middle-class or lower-class. Meanwhile, this particular neighborhood was the diamond in the rough.

It was also a gated neighborhood, adding to the snobbish nature of the area. The area symbolized the unwillingness to live with the rest of the population in Salinas. The attitude of the residents of the community also represented that idea. They were pompous and refused to go to community events. Heck, they didn't even share with others. To them, they were better than everybody else. Poetic justice was being served, however. During this rat infestation, the elites were on equal ground compared to their poorer neighbors.

The crew drove by the entrance and saw that the gates were open. That was a good sign that they were in the right place.

"Yes!" Otilia cheered,"

"I admit the gates being open is encouraging. However, it looks a bit empty here," Frank replied.

"Maybe everyone is deeper in the neighborhood," Otilia told Frank.

Meanwhile, in Clarke's SUV, Jessie was excited about getting out.

"Papa, is it really over?" She asked cheerfully.

"As I said, we can only hope so," he answered.

The crew drove through the gateway. Nobody was guarding the gate, which was alarming, especially to Frank.

"Nobody is guarding the gate. I've lived here for a while and that's unusual," Frank said.

"I don't think a guard is needed if this is an evacuation point," Jack replied.

"Frank is kind of right. Wouldn't someone be greeting us or telling us where to go?" Otilia was concerned.

Nonetheless, everybody went inside the neighborhood. When they entered, a couple of massive mansions greeted them. The mansion to the left was locked up completely, while the one to their right was open.

The crew was surprised that no one had tried to loot the mansion. With the invasion of rats, they figured many people were already dead. They drove around the neighborhood, only to find that it was empty. Nonetheless, they continued to drive toward the back, hoping to find activity.

However, their search was in vain. Clarke and Jack parked next to each other to assess the situation.

"Where's the staff for the evacuation?" Jack asked.

"As I suspected, this place is utterly deserted!" Frank shouted.

"Wow, thanks for stating the obvious. You must be fun at parties," Jack told Frank.

"Are we too late?" Clarke asked.

"I think we might be," Otilia said somberly.

"It's not even six o'clock yet!" Jessie shouted.

"I know, baby. Let me see if I can call my friend, Ben. He works in the National Guard. If this evacuation is legit, he can let us know what's going on," Clarke said.

Clarke used his satellite phone in his SUV to try to call his friend. Jack and the others were still impressed by the car phone.

Clarke tried to call Ben but wasn't getting a signal. He didn't hear a peep on the phone. He continued to try and call, but the results were the same.

"Damn, this isn't good. I can't get through to Ben. Either the signal is too weak or Ben has his phone off," Clarke told everyone.

"Why would he have his phone off? I'm unfamiliar with this technology. It's why I ask," Frank asked.

"The phone is only good when the battery of the car is good. Either there is no signal through the satellites or the more likely cause, the battery to his vehicle is dead. That also means... Ben might not even be alive anymore," Clarke tried not to break down.

"You ok, Clarke?" Otilia asked.

She went to hug Clarke to comfort him.

"It's just that Ben was one of the first people to greet me. He's the first ex-pat from the United States I met when I moved here. I had a hard time making friends out here before Frank was kind enough to introduce himself," Clarke said.

"I never met Ben before and I've been here most of my life," Frank replied.

"He works in the national guard, so he's not out much in public. When he was off duty, we would hang out by the market or the beach. He has a daughter who Jessie is close to. I just hope they're ok but fear they are not," Clarke answered Frank.

"Keep the faith, bro. He'll be ok. I'm sure he's a strong dude," Jack told Clarke.

"I believe that. There's not much we can do about it," Clarke told Jack.

"I could've sworn that this was where the evacuation was going to be!" Frank shouted, still dumbfounded.

He reached into his pockets to grab the note that he found in the police station. Frank read the note again and saw the date of April 12, 1985, which was the current date. Also, the time of deployment was at six thirty in the afternoon,

"See, we're supposed to be rescued," Frank said.

"Calm down, Frank. I was sure you weren't lying. The only thing I could think of was that they left early because the situation was worst than expected," Clarke figured.

Everybody walked around, not knowing what to do next. The reality was grim. They were running out of sunlight. It wasn't ideal to drive at night, but it was better than staying in the unoccupied neighborhood with the rats roaming around.

Frank saw a piece of paper blown by the wind. He grabbed it and started reading.

"A change of plans guys. The rats have been more aggressive than we previously thought. So we had to change the evacuation to April 11th, 1985 instead of the 12th. Besides, you elites are worth saving. You guys have the money to rebuild Salinas once it's destroyed by the rodents. We're sure we'll come up with an idea to kill off the killer rats and bring Salinas back.

When we bring Salinas back, it will be without those poverty-stricken hicks that resided here. It might be cruel to leave the general population out, but it will be so much easier for us to evacuate. I'm not too fond of planning a full-scale operation. Also, that means more goodies for you. So be sure to plan to leave this godforsaken land tomorrow. Best of all, nobody will be the wiser. As for these useless people, they can all die.

Regards,

Jose Moreno - Police Captain of Salinas

"It's just as I thought. We've been left for dead here!" Frank vented.

"Oh, don't start with that again," Jack replied.

"I wish I was joking, but read this!" Frank retorted.

Everyone read the note. They all realized that the police chief of Salinas had betrayed them. The man in charge of keeping Salinas safe had turned his back on everyone for his personal gain. Jack woke up to the idea that Frank was correct.

"It can't be. Guys, Frank is right. We have been left here to die," Jack admitted.

"It's about time you realized that. I'm sorry to say, but as I said, to the suits in San Juan, we're nothing but chewing gum. The kind of gum that has lost all its flavor and gets spat into the trash. Ha, even our police chief left us," Frank continued to vent.

"Yes, Frank, you are correct on all that. However, we can't dwell on that forever. It's not going to do us any good. We just have to find our way out. The only other place we can go to is Camp Santiago," Clarke replied.

"Isn't that a far ride from here?" Otilia asked.

"Not really. It's just tricky to get to, as the only way to get there is to take county road 3 back to Route 181. From there, we take the road north until we get to the camp. Could it be when we get there nobody around? Sure. However, it's our only real option," Clarke answered.

"It's better than standing in his deserted neighborhood," Frank replied.

"Believe it or not, I actually agree with Frank on this one. There's no use staying here," Jack told everyone.

"Ok, then, follow me. We'll have to get through the pole once again, but it should be a smooth ride after that. Come on while we still have some sunlight left," Clarke responded.

Everyone got into their respective vehicles. Jack would follow Clarke out of the neighborhood. The rain picked up in intensity again.

As the two cars reached the gate, a lightning bolt struck the breaker box next to the gate. The electric gate close in front of the crew.

"What the hell is going on? Why did the gate close?" Otilia asked.

"The breaker must have gotten overloaded and caused the gate to close automatically. Sadly, the gate wasn't wired to be fail-safe. It was wired to be fail-secured," Frank answered.

"What does that mean?" Otilia asked.

"It means we're stuck in here," Frank said.

"Nah bro, we gotta get that gate opened!" Jack replied.

"It's possible to open it manually. It's worth a shot. Come on!" Frank told everyone.

Everyone left their vehicles, trying to see if they could open the gate. When Jack touched the gate, he was electrocuted and set back. He fell onto the ground.

"That gate is filled with high voltage!" Jack shouted.

"The only way to turn off the power is from the mansion. I'll be damned," Frank said.

"How do you know this?" Otilia asked.

"I had a friend who worked on these mansions. This mansion to our left is the one providing power to the gate. We have to get inside and shut the power off. It's working on a backup generator inside. It's why there's power," Frank answered.

"We're going in there? You can't be serious!" Jessie vented.

"Sadly, there's no choice. That is unless you want to be stuck here forever," Frank replied.

Everyone was reluctant to enter the mansion. However, when they looked behind, a horde of rats entered the neighborhood.

"I think Frank is right. We don't have a choice. Let's go!" Otilia shouted.

Everyone ran from the horde. Without ammo for their weapons, they were unarmed to face the rodents. They rushed down the marble stairs. As they ran, they passed by statues of various Roman gods. It was indeed nothing like the humble neighborhoods in Puerto Rico.

They had no time to enjoy the beauty of the mansion as they were running from the killer rats. They saw the main wooden doors ahead. To their surprise, the doors were unlocked. They entered through.

Jack and Clarke slammed the door shut, then locked it to prevent the rats from entering.

While they were safe from the rats inside, there was a new danger. They were now in a closed location where rats had many hiding places. Nobody expected to be stuck in a mansion. It was a far cry from what was supposed to happen. However, everyone had to deal with it.

Chapter 15

The crew found themselves in an unfamiliar mansion. Jack looked out the window and saw the large horde of rats still outside.

"Well, the front door isn't going to be a wise escape route," Jack said.

"Right now, we need to stay focused on finding the generator powering the mansion and gate. If we can power down the gate, we can open it manually and get out of here," Clarke replied.

"And go where?" Otilia asked.

"We'll have to take our chances going to Camp Santiago," Clarke answered.

Everyone walked forward, staying close to each other. There was a large set of stairs just ahead.

"This mansion is huge. We can get lost easily," Frank said.

"Finding a map will help us in spades," Otilia replied.

"The smartest thing to do is to explore the mansion floor by floor," Jack told everyone.

"I agree. This mansion is also scary!" Jessie replied as she stood close to her father.

Oddly enough, the generator was still on. As a result, there was still light in the mansion. That gave hope to the crew that there were survivors in the house. On the other hand, there was no guarantee that any survivors in the mansion were friendly.

They walked towards the left, in the direction of the dining room. When they got to the dining room, they saw only the candles provided light. Nobody wasted time finding the switch.

Looking around the table, the crew saw a pork loin covered in maggots. Otilia and Jessie were ready to puke after seeing the larvae. Jessie knew that these maggots would eventually become disgusting flies. The same flies that would become a nuisance in the future. There was a foul odor coming from the pork lion. It was strong enough to cause Clarke to nearly puke.

Clarke wasn't a man who got disgusted easily. However, the pork lion looked to be on the table for a couple of days. It wasn't appetizing at all. The rotten pork was a slap in the face to the crew, who were feeling hungry. There were also pictures hanging on the wall. These were of some famous authors of the time.

There was a picture of Richard Ryan Rose to the left. He was popular for writing fiction surrounding Bigfoot. Next to him, there was Gareth Stevens, a British horror author. Finally, there was Anthony Castro. Anthony was a prominent horror comic book author.

"I recognize those guys. I'm a big fan of them. Guessing from the oil paintings, the people who live also love their horror," Jack said.

While the pictures look innocent enough, the crew found them to look rather creepy. There was nothing less appetizing than staring at authors who wrote some of the most gruesome horror stories while trying to enjoy dinner.

Besides the creepy pictures and rotten food, the dining room was quiet. Jessie then bumped into a gruesome discovery.

"Hey guys, you better take a look at this!" Jessie shouted.

It was the body of a butler. The body was dismembered and filled with many rat bites. A large pool of blood surrounded the corpse of the butler.

"This blood doesn't look fresh. Poor fella must have been dead for a couple of days," Clarke said.

"Eww... I can tell. There's a strong smell coming from him," Jessie replied.

"That's the smell of death. I'll say it's not a great smell at all," Jack confirmed.

"Why was the butler still here? Clarke asked.

"I got a better question. How did the rats get to him? Could it be that the rodents are already inside?" Frank asked.

Nobody had an answer. As everyone thought about what was going on, a rat crawled by the door to the main hall of the mansion.

Everyone heard a squeak but saw nothing around. Without any weapons, the crew hoped that it was just their imagination. Not wanting to stay in one place too long, the crew left the dining room. They headed through the next corridor, which led them to the kitchen.

Unlike the kitchen in the restaurant, this one had a terrible smell. Everybody thought it was rotten meat or another dead body inside. There was green blood splattered around the area. That caused concern that there were rats already hiding in the mansion. However, it was the smell that caused the most attention. The crew didn't find anything useful. There was no other door from the kitchen, so they headed back to the corridor.

Before they could leave the kitchen, a couple of rats attempted to ambush the crew. Jessie and Otilia screamed in panic as they were caught off guard. Clarke and Jack went for a couple of cooking pans. Frank got a pan for himself while protecting the ladies. The rats screeched as they prepared to attack the crew.

When the rats lounged at the crew, Clarke and Jack struck the attacking rats with their pans. More rats popped out of the oven, ready to attack them.

"Oh crap, more of these bastards?" Jack asked.

Frank saw his help was needed. He joined Clarke and Jack to attack the rats. They struck the rodents with their frying pans. Jessie saw there was a torch on the kitchen counter. It was used to make flambee for dessert. At that point, Jessie knew fire could be a good counter against the rats. She quickly grabbed the torch and rushed towards the horde.

"What are you doing? Do you have a death wish?" Otilia asked.

"No, I don't wish to die. Just watch!" Jessie answered.

Jessie turned on the small torch and let the flames out. The flames burned the rats. Jessie used up the torch until it was done. The flames burned right through the rats. What was a horde of rats was now a horde of barbequed rodents.

"Are you nuts! You're lucky the gas was off. We could have all been barbequed!" Clarke shouted at his daughter.

"Sorry, papa, but I couldn't let you fight all those rats by yourself," Jessie replied somberly.

"Don't be too hard on your daughter. She did save us," Jack said.

"True... To think I thought it would be safe in here. We gotta find that generator. Once that's done, we find a safe place to hide until morning. It's far too dangerous to drive out in the middle of the night," Clarke told everyone.

"My friend who worked on this mansion told me there was a 'safe room'. It was designed for the homeowners to hide in case there was a burglar inside. It's made out of pure steel. Not even the rats can break into it. However, I don't know where it could be," Frank responded.

"If I had a guess, it has to be in the basement," Otilia answered.

"Okay, we gotta get to the basement then," Jack said.

"Sounds like a plan," Clarke replied.

The kitchen still smelled like burned rats. At least, it was a tolerable smell compared to rotten meat. The crew left the kitchen and headed to the small corridor again. There were a couple of doors. One led to the butler's bedroom, while the other led to the basement. The door was labeled as such.

When they tried to open the door to the basement, they found it was locked.

"Son of a bitch, the door is locked," Frank said.

The lock had a crown symbol. That indicated that a special key was needed.

"If I had to guess, we have to find a key with a picture of a crown," Jessie said.

"Good observation... Now where could it be," Otilia asked.

"This mansion is huge. It could be anywhere," Frank answered.

The crew started by exploring the butler's bedroom, which was nicely kept. It was a small room with only a bed and two drawers to store clothing. There was a large closet as well to store bigger things. For a small room, it wasn't a living quarter for the butler.

They looked around for any keys but came up empty. Frank found what seemed to be a journal. He opened it and started to read. Most of the pages were filled with personal thoughts of the butler. However, it was mostly useless for the crew. That was except for the last page. They started to read it.

Butler's Journal

April 10th, 1985

For the most part, I've enjoyed working with the Rodriguez family for the past 15 years. It's hard to believe that I've been here since 1970. They've treated me well, I mean really well. I overheard them planning a surprise party for me. Honestly, I felt honored and loved. My father was wrong about the rich. Not all rich people are heartless. Heck, they even let me take a vacation when I want to.

There's one thing that's making me nervous. I've been hearing strange squeaking noises lately. Being here for 15 years, I found it odd that I've been hearing squeaking. I never thought of the mansion being filled with mice, let alone rats. I'm not a fan of rats. I don't know who is, though. Also, I've been hearing of strange deaths around the area. There have been bodies found dead. However, they weren't shot or stabbed. They were bitten to death. According to investigators, those bites were that of rodents. I never thought of rats being killers.

Another strange thing was the basement door being fitted with a new lock. I couldn't help but find that odd. After all, I never go into the basement except for washing clothes. Even then, I always asked Master Rodriguez for permission to go down there or at least let him know I was cleaning the bar. Most of the doors in the basement were locked. I mean the electrical room I get. However, there was one door that always got my attention. It's labeled as storage. The strange thing is that it has double locks.

I'm not the kind of person who will try to break into a room. My papa raised me better than that. Then again, I don't think Master Rodriguez is worried about me taking anything. I fear they might be a huge secret in there. Forgive me, father, but I intend on figuring out what is behind that door. I just hope it's nothing too bad, as I fear. The door to the basement needs the crown key. The master told me about it. He was vague about the location of the key but told me it was in his bedroom. Where in his bedroom? Who the heck knows? The master has this paranoia about locking lots of doors. Only a person who has something to hide is that paranoid. Could it be? I sure hope not.

I can understand why from a security standpoint. However, mansions tend to hold dark secrets inside. That or I'm simply reading too many horror novels. For now, I will believe the latter rather than the former.

When Frank was finished reading the journal entry, he had an idea where the key was.

"It looks like we're going on a wild goose chase for the key," Frank said.

"We have no time to waste. There's bound to be more rats waiting to eat us alive," Clarke replied.

Everyone headed back to the mansion entrance. They decided whether to go upstairs or continue investigating the lower floor. Splitting up was an option. Without any weapons, it was unwise for them to separate. Thunder was heard outside, along with a downpour. Jack looked out and saw it was raining like crazy. The rats that chased them inside were long gone.

However, with the gate closed, there was no way out. The crew had no choice but to continue investigating the mansion. Everyone decided it would be wise to head upstairs since that's where the bedrooms were probably located.

The crew started walking up the stairs. When they reached the middle of the stairs, a trap door opened below. Clarke and Jessie fell down the trap door. Jack pulled Otilia back before she fell.

"Clarke!" Jack shouted.

"I'm, ok, but it seems I ended up in the basement!" Clarke shouted back.

"Crap, we have to get to the basement to meet up with you. Just hang in there. We'll try not to take too long," Frank told Jessie and Clarke.

"We'll be ok, just get down here and make it snappy," Clarke replied.

"Yes, sir," Jack said.

Jack, Otilia, and Frank were still in the main hallway. With the hole in the stairway, they would have to find another way to the second floor.

Frank had a sick feeling that this house was more than just a mansion. He felt it was carrying a dirty secret. A secret that might explain why the rats were invading Salinas.

Chapter 16

Jack, Frank, and Otilia had to find another way to get to the second floor. As far as they knew, Clarke and Jessie were stuck downstairs. As they walked through the main hallway, they started to hear Moonlight Sonata by Beethoven play out of nowhere.

"What the fuck? There's music playing here?" Jack asked.

"That sounds like Moonlight Sonata. Unless this house is haunted, somebody is playing that song. There might be a survivor here," Frank answered.

"The question is, do we want to meet this survivor?" Otilia asked.

"Good question," Jack replied.

The music continued to play. Everyone found it strange that the Moonlight Sonata was being played to the perfect key. They were convinced that someone had to be in the mansion. The next room to the right of the main hallway was the living room.

It was a Tudor-style living room with wooden beams on the ceiling. There was a sofa set with a beautiful burgundy color. It matched the Tudor style of the living room and the mansion, for that matter. There was a marble table made in Italy. It had Roman-style columns on the corners. Frank was thrown off by the style of interior design. It was uncommon in Puerto Rico. Many people in Puerto Rico preferred the contemporary style of interior design.

Everyone looked around as Moonlight Sonata continued playing. The crew saw a nook next to a window. It was the perfect place to read a book. It was also the perfect room for a key to be located. As everyone searched the room, a couple of rats came out of the fireplace. Otilia heard the squeaking and turned around.

The two rats stared into her eyes, ready to pounce on her. She knew there was no room to panic. Instead, she backed away slowly. Jack and Frank saw the rats looking at Otilia. Jack ordered her to stay shut and keep the rats distracted. He grabbed a fireplace poker. Jack stabbed both rodents from behind.

"Whew, thank you, Jack," Otilia told him.

"Jack Childress, badass at your service. I'm always open to helping a beautiful belle out. You, my lady, are a beauty that needs to stay alive," Jack replied.

"Why thank you," Otilia said while her face blushed.

Frank looked at Jack with a face that spelled cringe. However, he kept quiet. That was until he realized that there was a fireplace in the living room.

"This mansion is strange, I'm convinced," Frank said.

"No shit, Sherlock," Jack replied.

"Why is there a fireplace in a mansion?" Otilia asked.

"Correct, this is Puerto Rico. It never gets cold out here. It's not like we're living in the hills, where during the winter, it does get down to the fifties or even forties at night. Here in Salinas, the lowest temperature is around sixty," Frank added.

"It might just be just for show," Jack said.

"Under a normal eye, yes. However, this mansion has shown us that it's anything but normal," Frank responded.

Frank smelled a strong burnt scent coming from the fireplace. He walked to it and studied it. As he smelled and looked at the fireplace, Frank could tell that it had been lit recently. Placing his hands on the back wall, he felt it was weak. Pushing on it, he felt some of the bricks falling apart. There was something off about the furnace.

"As I suspected, the wall behind the fireplace is ready to fall apart. That concludes my suspicion that this fireplace might be holding a secret. The wall has been weakened due to the flames of previous times the fireplace was set. If we can find a way to light the fireplace, it might weaken the wall," Frank told everyone.

"Wait a minute, are you suggesting there's a secret passage?" Jack asked.

"Look out the window. There's eight feet of wall sticking out. Nobody builds a wall that long for no reason," Frank explained.

"That could be where the key is," Otilia said.

"Possibly... I wouldn't put it past the homeowner to store the key in a secret area. This mansion continues to become more mysterious as we discover," Frank said.

Jack had a lighter, but it had no fluid. The crew kept the fireplace in the back of their head.

There were a lot of books surrounding spiritual sciences on the bookshelves. Otilia turned pale when she saw books about Santeria.

Santeria was a big religion in Puerto Rico that combined Catholicism and traditional African religions, including Voodoo. Otilia had terrible experiences with people who practiced Santeria. It had gained a bad reputation in Salinas for being a religion based on sacrificing and hurting others. Many people in Salinas were 'bible belt' residents. They were extremely conservative in their religious beliefs and considered Santeria a devilish practice instead of a religion.

She couldn't necessarily see the connection between the rats and Santeria. However, Otilia felt uncomfortable being in the mansion. The only thing that could have been plausible was that the elites were in that 'religion' and they infected rats with a virus to sacrifice the people of Salinas.

"What's wrong?" Jack asked Otilia.

"I see what's wrong. The owner of this house appears to have a strong interest in Santeria. I knew friends into that and let's just say their lives didn't end too well. Their relationships with their families were strained. After that, they experienced some bad luck until they mysteriously passed away. It's gotten a pretty bad reputation around here and within most of our people. I don't want to get too deep into it. What I will say is that there is the possibility that this house could contain some unsettling surprises," Frank explained.

"I see... So you think there might be some black magic involved with the killer rats?" Jack asked.

"I'm no expert on the religion. I keep my distance from stuff like that. What I will say is this house is giving me some bad vibes and it's not just the rats," Frank answered.

All of a sudden, Otilia feared that this adventure would begin to turn even darker. There was now the idea of a religion with a dark reputation entering the fray. When the crew finished investigating the living room, they couldn't find any keys. However, the fireplace caught their attention.

The fear was that Clarke and Jessie were stuck downstairs. If the homeowner was actually in the house hiding, there was no telling what he was capable of. Not to mention, the mansion was filled with killer rats. There was a corridor that led to a game room and the library.

The crew decided to explore the library first. As they entered, the lights started to flicker on and off.

"Crap, this is not good," Jack said.

"We better get to the basement as fast as possible before we get swallowed by this house," Frank replied.

They explored the game room. Again, it had a Tudor style just like the living room. There was a pool table, a ping-pong table, and a few arcade machines. It wasn't strange in any way. That was except, there was blood on the carpet. The blood went into the library. The scary thing was that the blood wasn't fresh.

Looking at the blood, it looked to be there a week ago. That suggested to the crew that there might have been a connection between the blood and the homeowner's religion.

"I'm scared!" Otilia squealed.

"I can't blame you. This house is giving me the creeps," Jack added.

"We might be bumping into a sacrifice house," Frank said somberly.

"Whoa, whoa! What the heck is a sacrifice house?" Jack asked.

"In Santeria, one has to sacrifice animals for blessings to be granted. Think of the Aztecs as an example. They used to do the same for the sun god. The host grabs animals such as goats or chickens and takes them to his 'house'. There he performs a ritual to complete the sacrifice. When that happens, the host should be granted a blessing. However, some blessings require more than just animals..." Frank said before getting cut off.

"Wait a minute. For those larger blessings, are you talking about human sacrifices?" Jack asked.

"In Santeria, only animals are permitted to be sacrificed. However, there are a lot of bad actors out there who use the religion to kill off their worst enemies. Some use Santeria as a smokescreen to hide the fact they enjoy killing others. It's a dangerous game we're playing just being here. I have a strong hunch that the owner of this mansion is a Santero," Frank somberly answered.

Jack held Otilia, who started to panic. They decided to follow the trail of blood into the library against their better judgment. Upon entering the library, they saw a horrific sight. There was a maid on the floor.

The poor lady was having her blood sucked by a horde of rats. None of the crew members had guns, so they needed to sneak around the rodents. They kept their cool despite the macabre execution of the maid.

The library was huge, spanning two floors. There were books in mostly every genre possible. It ranged from romance to horror and everything in between. The shelves were made out of the finest cherry wood. Again, this was unfamiliar to Puerto Rico as termites and ants were a huge problem on the island. Wood was not a good material to use on the island.

Frank continued to stay on the trail of the old blood. He believed that it might have led him to a secret passage. Jack took a quick detour to the corridor and saw there were double doors. They were locked, but the lock had a symbol of a sword. That meant another key needed to be found.

He quickly caught up with Otilia and Frank. Jack made sure not to get the attention of the rats. Frank continued to follow the trail of the old blood. It led them to a bookshelf that contained books about spiritual sciences. Jack and Otilia believed that it was a dead end. Frank, on the other hand, continued to look at the blood.

There was blood on a single book titled, "The Spirits Book". Frank grabbed it out of the bookshelf. When he did that, Frank saw the bookshelf open.

"Whoa, the classic secret bookshelf," Jack said.

"I got a bad feeling whatever is down there isn't going to be pretty," Frank told the crew.

Jack continued to hold Otilia's hand. Both of them were prepared to see the worst.

"Santeros usually commit rituals in the basement or places where they can have solitude. In short, we're about to see the true side of Mr. Rodriguez," Frank said.

Everyone went down the stairs. There was a musty smell in the stairway. When they walked down, they could hear their echoes. Torches helped light up the pathway. Water was heard dripping from the ceiling.

Nobody was particularly excited about finding out what was at the bottom of the stairway. Jack was expecting to see some weird voodoo stuff. They were in a corridor at the bottom of the stairs. Walking forward, they reached a metal door. They didn't open it right away. There was no telling if anybody was inside.

Frank stood next to the door without making any noise. He stood for a good five minutes. Frank was ready to open the door.

He opened the door slowly just in case. Frank peeked inside and saw it was quiet. Jack and Otilia followed him inside. When everybody went inside, they were greeted with a gruesome sight. There were lit candles around the room. Also, there were goat and horse heads. Otilia spotted dead chickens with their heads cut off. The room was filled with blood. It was truly a gruesome sight.

Dead rats were also found in the room. There was a large religious statue. Next to it, written in chicken blood, the wall read, "El poder de babalu aye!"

"What the fuck does that say?" Jack asked.

"Oh no, that is the babalu. That is the chief god of Santeria. My suspicions are confirmed. We're in the house of a santero. Translation, we better find a way out of this hell hole," Frank answered.

"There was a copy of the spirits book on a table. The table was also filled with hatchets, knives, and a bowl filled with goat blood. Everyone continued to feel disgusted.

It would only get worst. There were two cells in the back of the room. Both were filled with dead bodies. Otilia held her mouth in shock. The humans were bitten by killer rats and then placed in the cell to be 'sacrificed'.

"Hay dios mio... How can one be so cruel?" Otilia asked.

Frank looked around and saw more statues in perfect order. These religious statues were ones used in Santeria. The room was as disturbing as Frank thought it would be. There was a key in a chest that Jack opened. He grabbed it.

The key had a picture of a sword, which fitted the door that was locked upstairs.

"I found this key. This might help us get to the top floor," Jack told the others.

"Good find. We have to see what this crazy man is up to. I got a sick feeling that Clarke and Jessie might be in serious danger," Frank replied.

"Could that room that the butler was talking about in the basement be filled with dead bodies?" Otilia asked.

"It might be far worst than that. Not to mention, a part of me thinks this rat infestation was done intentionally. A lot of things aren't adding up for me," Frank answered.

As the crew investigated the room, Beethoven's Moonlight Sonata continued playing in the background.

Chapter 17

The crew looked around the underground room for anything else they could find. Jack decided to keep the fireplace poker. As for Frank, he found a metal bat. While a gun would have been useful, there wasn't one around.

Deafening silence was heard in the area. The only noise was the occasional water drop from above. Otilia looked around to see if she could find something useful to defend herself with. Instead, she found a note with bloody fingerprints. She told the men to read the letter with her.

Orders from Above

Carlos, as a fellow brother to the Babalu, you must complete your task. The rats were infected with a virus to enhance their ability. It was all an attempt for us to come up with the fountain of youth. However, the rats had a funny reaction to it. They've become aggressive. We can use that to our advantage, though. As the elites of the island, it's our duty to get rid of all the poverty-stricken heathens from Salinas.

By the power of the Babalu, Salinas will become the host city for him. We'll begin spreading our doctrine to those who survive the rats. To be honest, don't count on many people to survive. For those who survive, don't count on many to give in to the light. There are still those in Salinas who will resist us. Carlos, we want you to hunt down and if necessary, eliminate those who resist us.

The rats give us the perfect distraction. They will help cleanse the town of all these heathens. Soon Salinas will be our sanctuary. A sanctuary where the Babalu will bless us. We shall live in harmony with the great god himself. Perhaps the rats were needed to help us in our mission. Take care that they don't eat you alive. You're one of us, Carlos.

I and the other brothers and sisters are heading to San Juan. We're good friends with the governor up there. I can trust that he won't interfere with our mission. I wish you could come with us. However, you are needed in Salinas to ensure the cleansing process goes without a hitch. As a reward, you will be the grandmaster of the followers of the Babalu. We're so close to cleansing the world of all these heathens who want to believe in a fake god.

If anybody crosses your path, you have the license to kill...

Otilia was horrified by what she read. She believed the rat infestation was accidental, but the mass killing of people wasn't. She began seeing the killer rats were a result of evil people, looking for a new world order. Otilia always saw Santeria as a cult. This note simply proved it.

"This is horrible. How can people be so cruel?" Otilia asked.

"This isn't a religion. This is a fuckin death cult!" Jack retorted.

"Technically Santeria is a religion, but that's not saying much. I'm with you when you say it's a glorified cult. All I know is that this mansion is dangerous. Who knows if Carlos is still here, hunting us down," Frank told Jack.

"We need to find the others and get out of here!" Otilia told everyone.

"No, we can't just leave. I know it sounds crazy, but we need to find out if Carlos is here. If he's here, we need to stop him. There's no way I'm letting the babalu become our patron god. Salinas is a humble town, no need for a cult to take over," Frank replied.

"Good point. However, this cult has one thing, a lot of money and wealth. I'm concerned they have connections with high-ranking people," Jack said.

"You're right, Jack. They do have a lot of wealth. However, I was always taught by my papa that evil people never win. If we have to be the ones to stop them, so be it. If they start in Salinas, they are bound to expand until the entire island is theirs," Frank said.

"We have no time to waste then!" Jack responded, ready to leave the underground hell hole.

The three of them went up the stairs, ready to explore the rest of the mansion.

***

Clarke and Jessie fell into the basement. The ground was padded with a soft inflatable pad that broke their fall.

"Where are we, papa?" Jessie asked.

"That's what we have to find out," Clarke answered.

The two of them heard the music from upstairs. Jessie recognized that it was the Moonlight Sonata.

"I love that song. I wonder who's playing it?" She asked.

"It does sound nice, but I'm worried that someone else might be here," Clarke answered.

"That means there's another survivor,"

"Perhaps, baby. I just don't like this house. Who knows if we can trust this mystery person?"

Clarke was worried that something was off about the mansion. He had no idea that his suspicions were correct. They found themselves in a kid's playroom. There were Lego blocks, wooden blocks, teddy bears, and dolls. The room was painted sky blue.

The two of them looked around but didn't find anything useful. Clarke walked up to the door and opened it carefully. He looked around to make sure it was clear. When he saw it was quiet, he walked out. Jessie followed him to a large basement hallway. It was rather nice with wooden floors. Roman-style columns were holding the floor above.

On the wall, there were paintings of various battles of Ancient Rome. There was the battle of Cannae, the battle of Teutoburg Forest, the stabbing of Julius Caesar, and the sack of Rome. The paintings were worth at least hundreds of thousands of dollars.

As the duo looked around, they heard a squeak. When they looked around, there was nothing around. They thought a rat was around. There were many doors in the basement. Jessie saw a set of stairs to her left.

"Papa, I see stairs. I think we should catch up with the others," Jessie said.

Clarke nodded in agreement. The two of them walked up the marble stairs to the door. Jessie tried to open the door but found it was locked.

"Oh no! This was the door that was locked," Clarke said.

"So we're stuck here?" Jessie asked.

"I hope we can find a key, but if not, we better hope our friends can unlock it," he answered.

Downpours were heard falling from where they were. The sound of thunder was heard and it was loud. Jessie was startled by the lighting. Clarke comforted her by holding her. They went back downstairs.

There were about six doors to be explored. Not sure which to head to first, they headed to the left where they saw double doors. When they opened it, they saw a large bar with a poor table. Jessie and Clarke looked around to see what they could find.

Other than some beer and wine bottles, nothing was incriminating. There was a glass door that led back outside. They kept that in the back of their heads if they needed to escape. Out of nowhere, the sound of Beethoven's Symphony No.9 started playing through the speakers on the ceiling. Both Clarke and Jessie were startled by the subtle music.

"Holy shit, that scared me!" Clarke shouted.

"Shhh! Keep your voice down. Who knows if someone else is here," Jessie replied.

The light on top of the pool table turned on out of nowhere.

"This house gives me the creeps," Jessie said.

"Calm down, baby. This is not the time for us to panic," Clarke replied.

As they continued to explore the bar, they found the wine cellar behind the bar area. Looking inside, it was quiet. Once again, they heard a squeaking noise. Just like last time, it proved to be a false alarm.

They didn't find anything useful, so they left the bar. Back in the hallway, they decided to open the next door. It read 'electrical room'. When they tried to open it, however, it was locked.

"Makes sense that it's locked," Clarke said.

"We gotta keep exploring then," Jessie replied.

They decided to skip the next double doors, as they feared it was a trap. Instead, they headed to the next door, which was just a bathroom. There were more doors to open. The next door was a single door without a sign. When Jessie opened it, she saw a huge rat. She couldn't help but scream at the sight of such a rodent. Jessie fell on her butt.

"Oh my god, it's a giant rat!" Jessie shouted.

Clarke saw that the rodent wasn't moving. He felt something was off. When he walked inside, Clarke saw that it was nothing but a closet with a painting of a giant rat.

"Clever, it's just a painting of a giant rat. Nothing but a jump scare," Clarke said as he comforted his daughter.

"Who the heck paints a picture of such a hideous animal?"

"The homeowner is probably someone who isn't normal."

After the jump scare, Jessie got back on her feet. The two of them resumed exploring the rest of the basement. The doors on the other end were nothing but bedrooms.

The first bedroom they saw was that of the maid. It was a small room, but the bed was of the highest quality. Just like the dining room, it had a Tudor style to it. There was a painting of the city of Rome back in its glory. It seemed that Carlos had a thing for Roman history.

The walls were made from cedar wood. Once again, not a popular choice in Puerto Rico. For a rich homeowner, that wasn't an issue. The room even had a glass door that led to the backyard, again something that was not usual.

Clarke and Jessie saw the rain falling heavily. They kept the room in mind in case they needed to rest. When Jessie looked outside, she saw a horde of rats when the lightning struck the ground. As long as the rats were outside, she didn't fear. However, that didn't take away the fact they were just staring at her with their green eyes.

"We can't stay here, papa. Take a look outside."

"So I see. We'll just have to keep exploring."

The classical music was still playing in the background. Jessie decided to skip exploring the other bedroom. Instead, she decided to go for the other double doors that she skipped.

When Clarke opened the door, the lights were off. Jessie found the light switch and turned the lights on. Clarke closed the door behind him in case any rats were in the basement.

The two of them turned around and saw what the room was. They were in complete shock.

"Oh my... what is this?" Jessie asked in disgust.

"It looks like a torture room. Lord have mercy," Clarke answered.

The room had many torture devices that were popular in medieval times. Also, there were candles of varying colors that were lit. Catholic statues were found on a table with a red candle lit in front of them.

As they continued to walk forward, it only got more gruesome. There was goat blood in a pale. Neither Clarke nor Jessie understood the reasoning. They had no idea this was the room where rituals took place. There were also cells where dead carcasses were stored or where live animals would be stored to be killed later.

"This has to be some voodoo stuff," Jessie said.

"I'm no expert on that. Whatever this is, scares the crap out of me,"

There was a door further down the room. The two of them were almost scared to go through. Both of them figured that whatever was beyond that door was even worse than what they had just seen.

Before they could move forward, the door behind them slowly opened. A mysterious figure pulled out a dart gun and shot at Clarke. The dart struck him on the neck and put him to sleep immediately. Jessie saw her father hit the ground.

"Papa, are you ok? Wake up!" Jessie shouted as she shook her father.

She got no response. The mysterious figure walked into the room and approached Jessie from behind. It had a cloth that it applied chloroform onto. The mysterious person walked slowly up to Jessie and grabbed her. The person placed the cloth on Jessie's nose.

Jessie tried to break away but couldn't. After a couple of minutes of inhaling the chloroform, Jessie fell asleep next to the mystery person. Both Clarke and Jessie were asleep on the floor. The person picked Jessie up and took her to the next room. After that, the person transferred Clarke to the same room.

***

Jack, Otilia, and Frank finally got back to the library. When they got to the ladder, they saw that the maid's body was still there. The rats were no longer there.

What the trio didn't know was that Clarke and Jessie were in serious trouble. Carlos might have still been in the house, trying to complete the task given to him. Time was of the essence to save their friends.

Chapter 18

Jack, Otilia, and Frank had no idea Clarke and Jessie were in serious trouble. They were back in the library. The body of the dead maid was still on the floor. They checked the body of the woman and found she had nothing on her.

"Those rats ate her up completely!" Otilia said in shock.

"Yep, those rats are merciless. We better get to the basement quickly before anything happens to Clarke and his daughter," Jack replied.

"I got a bad feeling we're not the only ones in this mansion. That sick bastard, Carlos, might be here. I must admit an enemy we don't know is scarier than even these rats," Frank said.

"Why do you say that?" Jack asked.

"We don't even know who Carlos is. Not to mention, he is probably a Santero. Those people are bound to do just about anything to get what they want. If he had no trouble sacrificing a human close to him, he'll have no problem killing us. Furthermore, he won't just shoot us with a bullet. He'll make sure we feel the pain until we perish," Frank answered.

Otilia swallowed after hearing Frank's explanation. The crew left the dusty library. Jack grabbed the key he got from the underground area. He used it to unlock the door.

He opened the door carefully and peeked inside. When he saw the coast was clear, Jack ordered the other two to follow him. The crew saw they were in a Tudor-style hallway with many statues. There were also a couple of statues of men carrying pikes.

Everyone was confused as the mansion had Roman and Tudor-style rooms. They started to believe that Carlos was a mentally unstable man, who didn't know what he wanted. They looked outside from one of the windows. All they could see was darkness with trees blocking the view. It was still raining heavily.

The hallway was beautiful. Everyone saw the craftsmanship on the wooden moldings. Once again, this was against the norm in Puerto Rico. Wood was avoided like the plague due to termites.

Nonetheless, the crew couldn't stop being in awe of the hallway. Jack saw there were stairs on the other end of the hallway.

The path looked clear. However, as the crew knew, there might have been booby traps around the mansion. Despite that, Jack went ahead of the crew. When he reached the statue of the pikeman, Otilia saw the pike move.

"Jack, look out!" She shouted.

The pike was moving and ready to impale Jack. He had no idea that he had fallen for a trap. Otilia rushed toward him and pulled him back. The pike traveled across the hallway, barely missing Jack.

"Oh... I was about to say, why did you do that? But I see if you didn't I would have had a serious respiratory problem," Jack told Otilia.

"This dude is nuts! Booby traps as well? What other fucked up crap is in this house?" Frank asked.

Nobody answered as Jack went through the worst scare of his life. He got up from the wooden floor. The crew looked around a reading nook. There was a locked drawer that could easily be picked. With his lockpick, Jack began picking the lock.

With little effort, Jack was able to open the drawer. Inside there was a handgun with a spare clip. There was only one gun inside. With Otilia being the weakest of the three, she was handed the pistol. Despite being physically weaker than the men, Otilia was also really good with a gun.

"Try not to use it unless it's a real emergency," Jack told her.

She nodded her head. There was nothing else in the drawer. The crew left the reading nook and continued down the hallway. They heard squeaking coming from where they entered. When they turned back they saw the hall was empty. Only thunder was heard.

With the coast being clear, the crew decided to keep walking forward. Time was of the essence at this point. As they continued walking, a knight was holding a large double-bit axe. Otilia saw the stairs up ahead and became encouraged. When she wasn't paying attention, the axe began falling.

Jack saw his love interest about to be cut in half. He tackled her from behind as the axe was falling. The axe struck the wooden floor, but that was all it hit. Everyone breathed a sigh of relief.

After getting up from the floor, the crew had no time to gather themselves. A strong gust of wind blew out one of the stained glass windows. The rain started to blow into the hallway. However, that wasn't the only thing that made it into the hallway.

"Rats!" Jack screamed.

A small group of hungry rodents entered the hallway. Only Otilia was armed with a weapon. She didn't want to waste rounds on the rodents. There might not have been a choice, however. The rats started to rush at the three of them. Otilia didn't want to but had no choice. She fired a couple of rounds at two rats. Jack and Frank grabbed a couple of curtain rods that fell onto the floor to defend themselves with.

When the other rats closed in, Jack and Frank attacked the rodents. They swung their rods at the rats. The rods were too weak to kill the rascals right away. Otilia shot the rats when they landed on the floor. It cost her some valuable ammunition, but it was all about survival. The final rat got onto Otilia and bit her on the leg.

She fell on her knees and dropped the pistol. Jack heard her scream when she was bitten. He struck the rat with his rod. The rodent got off Otilia's legs, but the pistol was still on the floor. Frank quickly picked it up and shot at the mouse. However, he was a poor marksman. It took him three bullets to hit the rat.

"Whew, that was close," Frank said.

"Give me that gun. You can't shoot for shit!" Jack retorted.

"Well, I never had to use a gun, you know," Frank replied.

"I know. I'm just pulling your leg," Jack said while giving Frank and friendly punch to the shoulder.

"Otilia took a bad bite on her leg," Frank told Jack.

"You ain't kidding. Otilia, talk to me, are you ok?" Jack asked.

"That rat got me good on my right leg!" Otilia answered in pain.

"That looks pretty bad," Jack said.

"Diablo, ta mal ese. We need to cover that wound quickly. She'll be losing a lot of blood soon. Come on!" Frank said.

Frank was in a rush to find something to help Otilia. However, he missed another statue of a knight carrying an axe. Jack saw the axe ready to fall as he was caring for Otilia.

"Frank, duck back! That axe is ready to fall!"

Frank fell back as the axe missed him by only a foot. His face turned pale knowing he was that close to meeting his maker.

"Oh... man... that was too close..." Frank said.

Jack was worried about Otilia. In his mind, she couldn't die on him. This was his best chance at love. While she lost her husband not long ago, he knew she would be looking for a new man eventually. However, he didn't just want her for sex. Jack was actually in love with the woman. It was at an inopportune time, but Jack couldn't deny his feelings.

Otilia was in a lot of pain. Blood was pouring out of her leg. However, she knew she couldn't stay in the hallway. Frank saw the rest of the hallway was safe. He went ahead to see what was in the stairway.

Meanwhile, Jack helped Otilia up. Jack picked her up and started to carry her.

"Thank you, hun. You're not such a bad guy after all," Otilia told him.

"As I said, I want to protect the belle from any danger," Jack replied.

"I bet any woman would be lucky to have you, but I'm sure you're already taken,"

"Nope, still single. Hard to believe I know,"

"That is hard to believe. I'm sure any woman would have loved you. That accent of yours is too cute,"

"You mean my Tennessean accent? Oh, I was born with it, hehe. I'll take the compliment, though. I'm glad you find my redneck accent cute,"

"Hey, Jack. When this is all over, maybe we can go for a few drinks at a bar,"

"I would be honored, my dear belle. After this crazy adventure, we'll need to get loaded just to get back to normal,"

The two of them started to laugh. Frank, on the other hand, was concerned about finding something to cure Otilia. When he reached the stairway leading to the second floor, Frank saw another room to the right. It was the laundry room.

When Jack and Otilia reached Frank, they were startled when they heard a 1930's era song playing in the background. Nobody what song it was, but it sounded perfect for the setting they were in.

"This creepy music is getting on my nerve. I'm convinced that Carlos is a lunatic!" Otilia said.

"No kidding... Let's go to the laundry room. There's bound to be something to cure Otilia," Frank said.

Jack followed Frank into the laundry room. Unlike a laundromat in the neighborhood, this was a clean-looking room. The smell of suds was pungent, but it was a pleasant smell. The washing machines were state of the art for the 1980s, along with the dryers. Normally, the residents of Puerto Rico used the sun to dry their clothes, but Carlos didn't mind spending extra money for convenience. Oddly enough, the washing machines were on.

Frank shook his head but recognized that Carlos had money. Carlos could do whatever he wanted, even if it was pompous in nature. Jack placed Otilia on the marble floor. When Otilia was on the floor, Jack and Frank began searching for supplies. The old music was still playing over the speakers.

The song was romantic but didn't fit in with the setting the crew was in. If anything, it caused the crew to be more scared. It was the perfect music to swoop them into another jump scare. Another strange thing was that the machines were running with clothes. That raised suspicions that somebody other than them was inside.

Even the dryers were running. The crew wondered if they were being watched. There was nothing in the laundry room besides detergent and fabric softener. However, there was a medical room in the back. Nobody knew why there was one, but they were grateful for it.

Jack and Frank scoured the medical room for anything useful. There were some antibiotics and medical cloth, perfect to heal Otilia. The men came out with the supplies and started to treat Otilia. Jack carefully rubbed the ointment on her injured leg. Frank cut up the cloth that he needed to wrap the wound. As long as the bleeding stopped, Otilia would be ok.

Frank wrapped the cloth around Otilia's leg. She screamed but held in the urge to cry. Otilia knew there was no room for crying. After a few minutes, she carefully got up from the floor. Her leg was still in pain, but she sucked it up.

She was good enough to continue the journey. They left the laundry room with the music still playing. Before heading upstairs, they saw there was a door across from them. It was a beautiful cherry wood door. They would explore what was inside.

When they got inside, they found it was a personal office. Frank figured that it was Carlos's office. There was a 1700s-era cherry wood table with a typewriter on top along with a bunch of papers and a typewriter. A pungent ink smell was in the room. The crew believed when he wasn't a lunatic, Carlos might have been a talented writer. There were a bunch of manuscripts on the table. A couple of them were completed, with the others being incomplete.

There was also a bed that appeared to be used quite often. A window was next to the bed with the rain continuing to fall outside. It was quite the sanctuary. The crew looked for any clues in the room. There was a lot of material related to Santeria, which continued to creep out the crew.

Despite all of the material inside, there was nothing of importance except a key. The key had a tag named master bedroom. The crew knew it was time to go upstairs. With the mansion being booby-trapped, the crew knew it wasn't going to be an easy trip.

They still had no idea that their friend, Clarke was in danger of being killed in the basement. Before the crew left, Jack found a note that would change everything.

Chapter 19

The crew wondered what the note Jack had in his hand said. They all read the message together. It appeared to be a ripped portion of Carlos's journal.

Carlos's Journal 3/2/85

My new book is done. However, just like the others, it will probably be rejected. It's so hard to get a book published. Nobody understands my art. Many people believe I'm nothing but a warlock trying to push my beliefs onto people. Perhaps they're right, but that's why freedom of speech was invented. Sadly, here in Salinas, people also misunderstand my art. However, I understand why. They were raised in extremely conservative households and believed in a certain god.

I will always be grateful to my parents. They allowed me to embrace who I wanted to be. They allowed me to grow up how I wanted. I wanted to be a businessman and they fully supported that. It's a shame that they passed away too early before they could see my success. My father was into Santeria, just as I am. He taught me to be a santero.

People around here said my father passed away because of his religion. They believe it's nothing but a cult. All I have to say is that they're wrong! The poor fools have no idea how powerful the babalu can be if you fulfill his desires. Without him, I wouldn't have defeated my competitors and had the riches I have. I now live a life of luxury. To be fair, I would love a new wife. I'm getting bored with my wife. I want to have an adventure. Besides, she doesn't believe in what I believe in. I should have seen through that, but you know how love works. It's a powerful feeling that can cause us to make rash decisions without thinking. However, I have my own way of 'getting rid' of her.

I admit I had to do a lot of questionable things. Nonetheless, it works because I live a comfortable life. I want more people to follow me and worship the Babalu. It would change all of Salinas and Puerto Rico for the better.

But I know that's not feasible. There will be severe consequences for those who dare to get in my way. Whatever I have to sacrifice, I shall gladly obey. The babalu has ordered me to start experimenting on rats to clean up the filthy heathens when they are sacrificed. That would cut down on funeral expenses and be another way to make money from those too poor to bury their loved ones. Eventually, the end goal is to make Salinas a paradise for us, the elites, and those who worship the babalu. These non-believers must pay the consequences of remaining in the dark.

I'm not afraid to hunt for non-believers... This should be fun. They can be guinea pigs for my rats.

When they finished reading the page, they were in shock.

"Son of a bitch, so the rat infestation was intentional," Jack said.

"No thanks to being swallowed by this stupid religion or should I say, cult. This is why I'm so against Santeria!" Frank retorted.

"Oh my... Carlos purposely sent made a virus to infect rats so he could kill off all of Salinas..." Otilia was still in shock.

"Carlos is a sick bastard!" Jack replied.

"He might be sick, but that makes him that much more dangerous. Anybody willing to dig into the depths of a dark religion is a deadly enemy. We need to act quickly. Clarke and Jessie might be in real trouble. And it might not be the rats who get them," Frank told everyone.

With no time to waste, the crew left Carlos's office. They were back in the stairway. It was a beautiful stairway decorated with portraits and gold columns. Jack prepared to head upstairs. Frank stopped him.

"What's wrong?" Jack asked.

"This mansion is what's wrong. It's filled with booby traps. What makes you think that stairway is safe?" Frank asked his own question.

"Hmm... good point," Otilia asked.

"Until I see it, I don't believe it," Jack retorted.

Frank grabbed a bronze vase from the small table. He threw it on the stairs. When the vase landed on the stairs, the stairway opened up. Below the opening was a long fall to the basement.

"You were saying..." Frank told Jack.

"Good catch," Jack replied, feeling stunned.

"What do we do now? How do we get up to the second floor now?" She asked.

"If I wasn't seeing things, there was a ladder in the laundry room. We can use it to climb straight to the second floor and avoid the trap," Frank answered.

"Let's get that ladder then. The more we stay here, the more time we waste," Jack told Frank.

The crew walked back into the laundry room. The ladder was behind the dryers. It would be tough to get the ladder out as it was tightly inside. Frank saw it was a twelve-foot ladder, enough to get up to the second floor. As Frank started pulling the ladder, Jack and Otilia were ambushed by a few rats that popped out from behind the washing machines.

Jack was armed with the fireplace poker while Otilia grabbed a broomstick that was next to her. The killer rats started pouncing on the two. Otilia and Jack fought off the rats with their melee weapons. After that, they saw a few rats trying to attack Frank. They rushed toward the rats and attacked them. Otilia's right leg was still hurting and it was felt when she had to kneel.

Jack saw that Otilia was on the floor. He got in front of her, ready to take the brunt of the impact.

"You want her. You gotta get through me first!" Jack shouted.

Otilia was stunned when she saw Jack willing to risk his life for her. She saw the image of Ruben in front of her. She knew that Ruben would have done the same for her. At that point, Otilia figured it was wise to give Jack a chance when they escaped the hellish adventure. She had a gut feeling that Jack would be just like her late husband.

The rats started to lunge at him. Frank saw what was happening. He knew he couldn't just watch. He grabbed his stick and joined Jack in the fight.

"Nice of you to join us!" Jack said with a small smile.

"I couldn't let you take these bastards by yourself!" Frank replied.

Jack and Frank fought off the rodents as they protected Otilia, who favored her leg. After a minute of fighting, they had defeated the rodents. The once spotless laundry room was splattered with green blood.

The men checked on Otilia, who was favoring her leg.

"I'll be ok. I just can't put too much pressure on my leg," Otilia said.

"That's not good. How are you going to go up the ladder then?" Frank asked.

"I'll just have to go slow," she answered.

"Don't worry, Frank. Otilia is a strong woman, right honey?" Jack asked.

Otilia nodded her head. With the coast clear, Jack gave Frank a hand in removing the ladder from the back of the dryer. The men worked together to bring the ladder to the stairway. When they propped the ladder, they saw it wasn't quite large enough to go over the wooden railing. That meant they needed to climb over the railing from the ladder.

It wasn't the best idea, but the hole in the stairway was too big to jump over.

"I'm worried about Otilia. Her leg isn't in the best shape," Jack said.

"Tell you what, I'll go up first. Otilia will go second. When she gets close to the top, I'll pull her up. If she falls, you can catch her," Frank replied.

"Not a bad idea. That noggin is working overtime," Jack said as he tapped Frank's head playfully.

Frank and Jack placed the ladder onto the second floor railing.

"Ok, here I go," Frank said, as he started climbing the ladder.

Frank grabbed the railing to pull himself over when he reached the top of the ladder. He handed on the soft carpet below.

"Ok, I'm up. Come on, Otilia, you're next," Frank said.

"You'll be ok. I'll be here if you fall," Jack told Otilia.

"Ok, I'm trusting you to catch me," Otilia replied.

She started climbing the ladder. At first, the climb was painless. When she got close to the top of the ladder, her right leg gave away. It caused her to slip. Frank tried to grab her hand, but he was too short. Otilia slipped off the ladder, falling toward the floor.

Jack stopped her fall as he took the brunt of the impact. The important thing was that Otilia was ok.

"Whew, I thought you were lighter. You sure look thin," Jack told her.

"I did fall close to ten feet from the ground, hehe. Grab my hand. I'll pick you up," she responded.

Otilia was determined to get up to the second floor. She started climbing the ladder again. This time, she took her time to avoid putting too much pressure on her legs. The move paid off as she reached the top of the ladder. Frank grabbed both of her arms to pull her up. She climbed over the railing.

"Good job, honey!" Jack said.

Otilia smiled back at him.

"Is Jack trying to hit on you?" Frank asked.

"Perhaps and why does that concern you?" Otilia asked.

"Remember, you just lose Ruben. It would be a bit quick to jump into another relationship like that," Frank answered.

"I know you're looking out for me. I appreciate that, hun. However, me and Jack are just friends. We're not thinking about a relationship right now. Besides, we gotta survive this first," Otilia replied.

"It's not that. I think you and Jack would make a great couple," Frank said.

"Really? That's sweet of you to say. How about you? I know your wife passed recently," she told him.

"Yeah, but honestly, I'm not ready for a relationship. At least not a new one. Anyway, here comes Jack. Let me give him a hand," he replied.

"I'll help you!" Otilia said.

Frank and Otilia helped Jack up to the second floor.

"Thank dudes! Now that we're on the second floor. It's time to find the master bedroom. Hopefully, that will lead us to the key to get downstairs," Jack said.

"I'm almost afraid to see what is downstairs," Otilia replied.

"That would be an understatement. We've already established that Carlos is mentally unstable," Frank told everyone.

The crew started to walk through the hallway. It was darker than the hallway downstairs. The lights were dimmed down. There wasn't a switch to bring up the brightness. It was controlled remotely. The walls had beautiful reddish wallpaper with Tudor flowers on it.

There were a few doors in the hallway. The first one they opened was a closet with a picture of a killer rat. Everyone jumped scared, thinking it was a real rat. After a few seconds, they realized it was just a jump scare.

"Now I know this dude is sick!" Jack said.

There was nothing of importance in the closet. The crew saw another door behind them. As they opened the door, soft 1930s-era music continued playing in the background. Behind the door was a picture of the babalu. Below was a message in Spanish saying, "The Almighty Babalu shall rule the known world!"

It was written in red. Upon further inspection, the crew saw that it was written with blood.

"Oh lord... I just hope this isn't human blood," Otilia said.

"Knowing Carlos, it might just be. If I was a betting man, this might be his wife's blood," Frank replied.

"You might be right. He did mention that he had his way of dealing with her. My god, this might be how he did it... Poor woman..." Jack somberly said.

"As I said, santeros don't care who they hurt. As long as they are 'blessed' by the babalu, they will do anything. Even murder their wife," Frank told the others.

"I can't wait to get my hands on this lunatic!" Jack shouted.

"I think we can all agree with that," Frank replied.

When they walked into the room they saw religious statues including one of a large bloody hand. Jack wondered what that represented.

"That hand represents the five African powers in Santeria," Frank told Jack.

The room creeped out the crew and they left quickly, finding nothing useful.

They continued walking forward until they reached the stairs leading to the main hallway. On the other side of the hallway, there were two doors. They decided to open the door to their left.

Upon opening the door, they saw a research office. Inside there was a fish tank filled with water. There were insect specimens on the wall as well. There were books on genetic engineering and science on the left side of the room. There was a table filled with papers. Most of them were related to mutating rats, which was disturbing enough.

However, the most disturbing thing on the table was what was found on the right side. There was a ripped note that caught Otilia's attention. She gathered the men around her. They figured there were more clues on the note.

A Random Note from Carlos's Journal

My wife is lovely, but she doesn't have the same beliefs as I do. That hadn't bothered me for a while. However, the more I'm learning, the more I'm concerned that she might hurt my chances of obtaining the ultimate blessing. The deeper I look, the more I find that me and her have little in common. While that makes me sad, it opens my eyes to what needs to happen.

I've tried to teach my wife the wonders of Santeria. After all, if a santero can get his family to join him, he or she will only become stronger. On the other hand, he or she will get weaker if their family is against them. The decision of what to do with her has been killing me inside. I must remember one thing. She didn't give me the ability to unlock all these riches. No, that was by the power of the babalu!

The choice is becoming clear on what I need to do...

(The rest of the note is ripped)

"Wait a minute, the rest of the note is missing," Otilia said.

"My guess is that it was the most incriminating part of the note and Carlos needed to cover his ass," Jack replied.

"I'm sure I know what happened to his wife. That blood on the wall might have been hers," Frank told the crew.

Otilia backed away in fear. As she backed away, her hand accidentally hit a secret button below the insect specimens. When the button was pressed, the bookcase on the left side of the room moved towards the back part of the room. There was a small hole behind the bookcase.

Inside the hole, there was a .357 magnum with some extra ammo. Also, there were a couple of magazines for a pistol. Otilia saw they fit her gun. Nothing else was inside, but the crew was a bit better armed. After exploring the office, they left to explore the final door. It was decorated with the Rodriguez family emblem. Jack figured that it had to be the master room.

He inserted the key and turned the lock. The door opened. It was indeed the master room. What was inside would shock everyone.

Chapter 20

The crew walked into the bedroom and was shocked to see the corpse of a female. She appeared to have been bitten by killer rats. At the same time, there were red and white candles surrounding her. The candles were placed in a perfect circle around the female.

"Oh no!" Frank said.

"What's wrong? Besides the fact there is a dead woman on the bed," Jack asked.

"Don't you see the candles around her? This had to be a ritual. I fear this might be Carlos's wife. She was probably sacrificed," Frank answered.

"No... that means the words written in blood might have been hers. I don't know if I can take any more of this," Otilia replied.

"It's probably her blood. We need to search this room for the key and fast. I have a sick feeling Clarke and his daughter are in serious trouble!" Frank told the crew.

Everyone started to explore the room. It was a beautiful room with a 1700s-era bed. The wallpaper was a peach color. There was also plenty of Tudor-era furniture. Carlos appeared to be a collector of Tudor history. Frank failed to see the connection between Carlos's obsession with the Tudor era and his Santeria beliefs.

The only thing he came up with was that all of this was a cover for Carlos's true nature as a person. Everyone was looking for a key to help them reach the basement. Jack, on the other hand, kept his eyes out for lighter fluid or a lighter.

He still remembered the odd fireplace in the living room. If he could light up the fireplace, perhaps he could knock the wall down. Jack suspected there was a secret room behind the fireplace.

The sound of squeaking was heard as everyone searched through the bedroom. Just like the other times, it was a false alarm. However, the crew knew that rats were nearby. They looked through drawers, as the butler said in his note. Other than disturbing prayers and a hit list of people, the crew didn't find anything. However, the hit list was disturbing enough that the crew turned pale.

They were dealing with a man willing to take innocent lives to please his pseudo-deity. The problem for the crew was that they couldn't find a key or a lighter. Jack looked up and saw a part of the ceiling that was unlike the rest. It was a square shape. He figured there might have been a secret passage above.

There was a small stepladder that he took. Jack climbed it and saw a small rope on the ceiling. He pulled it and the ceiling opened. Also, a ladder came down, revealing a secret passage above.

"I should have known that there was a secret passage above. I'll go up alone. You guys make sure the room is safe from any rats. Also, who knows if our crazy lunatic is hiding in the mansion somewhere," Jack told Frank and Otilia.

"Be careful up there," Otilia told Jack.

Jack climbed the ladder. When he closed in on the top of the ladder, the bottom of the ladder cracked in half.

"Son of bitch!" Jack said.

"We'll be here to catch you," Frank replied.

"Ok, I'm counting on you. Let's see what Carlos has hiding up here," Jack responded.

Jack started to explore the area above the master bedroom. He found lots of candles, religious statues, and a large drawer. The drawer was locked. Jack used his lockpick to unlock the drawer. Inside the drawer was some lighter fluid. It wasn't much but enough to get the fireplace lit up.

Before Jack could get back down, there were a couple of killer rats trying to ambush him. He used the fireplace poker to kill both rodents. There was no need to overkill with the magnum. As Jack was heading back to the ladder, he looked to his right and saw a giant rat.

"Holy shit! No wonder why the rats can repopulate," Jack said.

"What's going on up there?" Frank asked.

"There's a giant rat up here," Jack answered.

"Get back down here!" Otilia shouted.

Jack was tempted to shoot the giant rat but didn't want to take the chance of being unable to kill off the rodent. He decided that it was best to leave it alone. Jack carefully made his way to the hole, avoiding giving attention to the giant rodent.

There were a bunch of rats feeding off the giant rat. In his mind, Jack felt the best thing to happen to the mansion was to destroy it. That would kill all the rats and halt the production of the virus-infected rats. Jack didn't go down the ladder immediately.

"I'll catch you, Jack," Frank said.

"I got a better idea. Frank, take the mattress off the bed, and put it below me. That way, I can jump down and have a soft place to land," Jack replied.

"Ah, did you forget? There's a dead body on the bed! There's no way I'm touching that corpse, sorry man," Frank retorted.

"I have to agree with Frank. Who knows what bacteria or virus could be on that body," Otilia said.

"Fine... ok, Frank, make sure you catch me. If I break my foot, it's your ass!" Jack told Frank.

Frank positioned himself right below the hole. Jack started to go down the hole. He took a deep breath and dropped below. Frank caught Jack easily. The impact of the fall caused Frank to hit the carpet. However, it was better than Jack potentially hurting himself.

"You ok?" Frank asked.

"Yep, good catch. However, what is not good is the situation we're in," Jack replied.

"Oh, I know we're in a hell hole," Frank told Jack.

"No, it goes further than that. The giant rat up there is breeding new rats quicker than we can kill them. The only way to clear all this up is by destroying the house," Jack replied.

"But how are we going to destroy the house?" Otilia asked.

"There's the million-dollar question. It's not like we have C4 on us," Jack answered.

"I hate to say it, but the best course of action is to find Clarke and his daughter, then just get the fuck out of this place. I'll miss Salinas, but if I have to start somewhere else, it is what it is. As far as I'm concerned, my beautiful town is screwed," Frank said somberly.

"Frank, don't give up. There's bound to be somebody in power who will listen to us and not let these elites get away with this," Otilia told him.

"I fear that many of the higher-ups are in the Santeria religion. We might be fighting a losing battle. At this point, we need to worry about our survival. As much as I want to save my neighborhood, it might not be possible,"

Frank was distraught about what was happening. Jack realized that Frank did have a heart and cared. He went to hug him.

"It's ok, bro. You're right, there's not much we can do. However, I still want to take Carlos out. If we can eliminate one cult member, it's a start," Jack told Frank.

"Agreed," Frank replied.

Jack carefully inserted the lighter fluid into his lighter. It wasn't a lot, but he didn't need much. When the fluid was in the lighter, Jack tried it and the lighter worked.

"Sweet, we got a working lighter. Now we need to get back to the fireplace. I'm sure the key to the basement must be in that area," Jack told the others.

Before they left, a horde of rats came down from the ceiling and surrounded the crew. Otilia and Jack didn't want to waste ammo on the rodents. Instead, they rushed out of the master bedroom and locked the door to trap the rats inside.

"Whew, that was close," Otilia told the guys.

The crew knew it wasn't wise to stay in the hallway in case the rats broke out of the bedroom. They rushed to the main stairway. While the stairs were booby-trapped, the crew rode down the banister to the first floor. Upon reaching the lower floor, they heard the master bedroom door open.

"Crap, the rats broke through. Quick! To the living room before they can find us," Frank shouted.

Everyone rushed to the living room. Jack wasted no time lighting up the fireplace. Otilia kept an eye out for any rats that might have come down. She was relieved when she saw no rats around. Frank saw the wall behind the fireplace weakening when the fireplace was lit.

Otilia grabbed an iron pipe and handed it to Frank. As the fire burned, Frank struck the back wall of the fireplace. The wall started to crumble. He continued hitting the wall until the hole was big enough for a human to fit in. Jack went to the bathroom and grabbed a pale with water to shut off the fire. The crew saw a huge hole created after the fire was extinguished.

Jack got on his knees and peeked inside. He saw it was an actual room on the other side.

"What could be inside?" Frank asked.

"That's what we're about to find out," Jack answered.

The three of them crawled through the hole and entered the secret room. Upon entering, they saw a door leading outside to a secret passage.

When they looked through the rest of the room, they were horrified. There were goat, horse, and cow heads on a table. Otilia was terrified. Even the strong willed Jack cracked when he saw the animal heads on the table. On the right side, there were dead chicken carcasses without their heads.

There was a statue of the Babalu, covered in blood. There was a prayer book with bloody fingerprints. On the left side of the room, there were hatchets, knives, and other torturous-looking weapons. Behind them, there were bead chains of various colors. Santeros would put these beads on based on what class they were. This strengthened Frank's idea that Santeria was nothing more than a cult.

Everyone wondered, what was worst, the rats, or the satanic practices taking place in the mansion. The adventure was getting darker as they went. The door leading out was locked with a double deadbolt lock. Without the key, opening the door was out of the question. The windows were guarded by steel bars on the outside portion. It was safe to say this room was not meant to be visited by anyone outside of Carlos.

The crew looked all over the room and attempted to find a key or something. They weren't worried about rats getting in at the moment. However, they did find some dead rat carcasses that were probably experimented on.

"Carlos is one sick bastard," Jack said.

"You said it. I can't wait to take him down," Frank replied.

As they continued searching, Otilia found a key with a crown on it on the key hanger next to the door.

"Guys, I found the key," Otilia told the crew.

"Good, now we can get to the basement. Hopefully, Clarke and Jessie are ok down there," Jack replied.

The crew continued to search for any more clues. They would find drums and other musical instruments. The musical instruments were used during Santeria gatherings and rituals. Many African rhythms were used during these events. There was a closet that they checked. Inside there were many traditional African garments used by practitioners.

The colors were beautiful, ranging from yellow to red in different patterns. However, that was overshadowed by the person who would wear them. The crew realized that Clarke and Jessie were probably in dire need of help. They crawled out of the room and headed back to the living room.

The adventure had gone from a crazy rat infestation to a sinister plot to bring a new religious order to Puerto Rico. With the crown key, it was time for Frank, Otilia, and Jack to head downstairs. The horrors in the basement would prove to be far worse.

Chapter 21

The crew walked toward the kitchen on the first floor. When they reached the kitchen, the crew headed to the corridor where the door to the basement was. Otilia used the key to open the door to the basement. There was a set of stairs that led down.

As the crew walked downstairs, the rain continued to pour. Frank was concerned that the continuous rain would cause massive flooding. If the roads were flooded, getting to Camp Santiago would be challenging.

Jack had the magnum at the ready, while Otilia had the pistol armed. Everyone walked down the stairs slowly. They believed that Carlos was in the basement. So they wanted to be quiet. Some squeaking was heard in the hallway. Once again, it proved to be a false alarm. A strong gust of wind blew, causing the window to shake.

Otilia thought that the force of the wind would break the window. However, the window stood intact. Nonetheless, the wind was enough to shake the crew.

"Ok, guys, we gotta find Clarke and Jessie," Jack said.

"I would say to split up, but in this hell hole, that wouldn't be a smart idea," Frank replied.

"Agreed," Otilia responded.

The three of them remained together as they started to explore the basement. First, they explored the left side of the hallway. There was the door to the electric room that was locked. Jack tried to pick the lock but found it was locked with a complex lock.

"Fuck, this door is too hard to pick. It makes sense, though. It's the electrical room. Carlos wouldn't want anyone messing with the house. We'll need a key to get in," Jack said.

"I don't think Clarke and his daughter are inside," Frank told Jack.

"I know that genius! It's about cutting the power off from the gate or did you forget already?" Jack retorted.

"Oh, yeah... sorry," Frank said in a low tone.

The next room they entered was the bar. It was empty, with some green blood spattered around. The crew got a bit nervous seeing the green blood on the floor. However, they also saw dead rats on the ground. Also, there wasn't any human blood.

The suspicion was that Jessie and Clarke were in the bar already. Everyone continued to investigate the bar. Jack saw a variety of booze on the counter behind the bar. Considering the adventure he was going through, he was thinking about a drink.

While Frank and Otilia continued to look around the room, Jack helped himself to the bar. He grabbed a bottle of Jack Daniels and poured himself a shot. The other two turned and saw Jack helping himself with liquor.

"Dude! We're in the middle of a life or death situation and you're helping yourself with... Jack Daniels," Frank was shocked to see the Jack Daniels bottle.

"My man, we've been through a lot. The least we can do is enjoy a shot. Who knows, it will probably calm us down. It's been a while since I had myself a shot anyway. Care to join me?" Jack asked.

"Considering it's Jack Daniels, I can't deny myself a drink. Pour me one," Frank answered.

"You want it straight?" Jack asked.

"Is that supposed to be a trick question?" Frank asked.

"Hehe, yep. I needed to make sure you knew that whiskey is meant to be drunk straight. Cheers, dude. We're on our way to survival," Jack answered.

Otilia looked at the men drinking their shots. She was concerned they would start drinking and lose sight of the mission.

"My beautiful belle, feeling thirsty?" Jack asked.

"No, I don't drink. I hope you two aren't planning to drink that entire bottle. You know we're still stuck in this crazy mansion, right?" Otilia asked.

"Calm down, hun. We're just taking one little shot. Come on, try it," Jack answered.

Otilia wasn't a drinker. She tried liquor back in the day and hated it. However, she wanted to make a good impression on Jack. She was starting to gain feelings for him. Otilia decided to give in and have a shot.

"Ok, Jack. You win. Pour me a drink," Otilia told him.

"Now you're talking. You're in for a rush!" Jack replied.

Otilia prepared to drink the shot. She had a feeling that she was going to taste terrible. However, she was pleasantly surprised.

"This is actually good!" Otilia said.

"Told ya," Jack replied.

"As good as this is, I think Otilia is right. We need to stay focused. Once we're safe, we can drink like the drunkards we truly are," Frank told Jack.

"Ughh... ok. I guess you're right. Let's continue our investigation," Jack replied, feeling defeated.

The crew walked into the wine cellar and saw nothing inside. There were no signs of Clarke or Jessie. When the coast was clear, the crew headed back to the bar. When they left the cellar, two rats popped out of the vent. They attempted to ambush the crew from behind.

Jack heard a small chirp from behind. He quickly turned around and saw the rats coming from the wine cellar.

"Lookout!" Jack warned the others.

Otilia quickly turned and shot both rats before they could get any closer. She blew on the gun. The men were impressed by her skills with the pistol.

"Nice one! I thought the rats had a jump on us," Frank told her.

"It might be the liquor kicking in," Jack joked.

"Doubt it, but who knows," Otilia replied as she winked toward Jack.

Jack took that as her possibly being interested in him. However, he didn't push his luck. With the bar proving to be quiet, the crew walked back to the hallway.

When they reached the hallway, they saw a locked double white door. The door looked important. Jack was unable to pick the lock. As a result, the crew now had to find two keys. They skipped that door and headed for the door next to it. When they opened the door, they were greeted by another jump scare. It was the same picture of a giant rat that Clarke and his daughter saw.

"Calm down, guys, it's just a picture," Frank said.

"Man, does that look so damn real!" Jack shouted.

"Keep your voice down! We don't want Carlos to know we're here," Frank whispered loudly.

The crew continued down the hallway until they reached the next door. It led them to a maintenance room. The crew looked around for a key. However, they found no such thing. There were plenty of tools, but they were useless for the crew's needs.

They left the room and headed to the right end of the hallway. When they reached the right end, they entered the maid's bedroom. Upon entering the bedroom, they saw it was well-kept. With the maid already dead, the crew was free to explore the room. While they searched for a key, Otilia found a note in a drawer.

She gathered everyone to read the message. She hoped it would provide a clue.

A love note to Carlos

Mi amor, te quedo mucho!

I can't stop thinking of you. I know you're married. At the same time, I'm aware you're having a tough time with your wife. You haven't told me personally, but I can tell that you don't love your wife. Normally, I wouldn't step in with a married man. This time it's different.

There's something else you need to know. I know you're a santero. No worries, I'm into Santeria myself. If you desire to get rid of your wife, you can count on me to help you. Besides, I believe you need a partner who believes in the same thing. Your wife will only hold you back if you stay with her.

Not to mention, I think you're delicious. I want to have you in bed. I can wear my sexy maid outfit with 5-inch high heels and black pantyhose. I'll be a naughty maid, just for you. I can turn your world upside down, in a good way of course. To grow your spiritual family, you need people who believe in the same thing. As lovely as your wife is, she doesn't fit the description of a devout follower.

I know where I can get a gun. So we can do the task quickly. I have one in my house. If you wish, I can kill her for you. After that, we can perform a ritual. We can always say that she needed to be sacrificed. Once that is done, we can live our lives together forever. Don't deny the fact that you have feelings for me. I think you're hot! I'm feeling wet just thinking about you. I love to dress naughty for you. It's been a long time since I've had these kinds of feelings for anyone.

Besides, I enjoyed that long passionate kiss you gave me in the kitchen. I felt so hot. I wanted to take everything off right there and then.

I'll await your reply, my love.

Carla

The crew found out that there was a secret plot to kill Carlos's wife. Also, he might have been having an affair with the maid. However, by the look of the message, it never reached Carlos. The paper was still untouched. Either that or the maid got cold feet with her plot to get with the man.

It really didn't matter as the maid was found eaten by a horde of rats. Also, Carlos's wife was lying on the bed, bitten by rats with candles around her. Otilia was sick to her stomach with what she read. Frank feared that Carlos might have killed his wife on his own will.

At the very least, the crew knew this mansion held lots of dark and deadly secrets. As they looked around the room, they found a key. It didn't have a tag on it. Nonetheless, they took it. The key had to open something.

They investigated the room further. It proved futile as nothing more was found. When Otilia looked out of the window, she saw the squeaking come from a few rats that were outside. She breathed a sigh of relief.

The crew left the bedroom filled with dark secrets. The first door they tried opening was the electrical room. While the key went into the lock, the door did not unlock.

That meant the double white door had to be what the key unlocked. Otilia was nervous about unlocking the door as it was the door described by the butler with extra security. She knew that a lock like that wasn't just put on any random door.

There had to be something inside that Carlos didn't want anybody to know. Boy, would she be right in more ways than one.

Chapter 22

Otilia turned the key on the lock. The crew was ready to see what was inside the room the butler was talking about in his journal. Before going inside, they looked behind them to make sure there were no rats.

There was a small horde of rats that came down the stairs.

"Trying to get the jump on us, heh?" Jack asked.

Jack and Otilia saw the rats heading their way. Wasting no time, they shot at the mice, killing many of them. Both of them had to reload their weapon. Frank saw a rat lunge at the two of them. Instead of standing around, he jumped in front of the rat and struck it with his stick. Frank impaled the rodent, killing it for good.

When the horde was defeated, the crew checked to see if there were no more rats around. The coast was clear, so they continued walking. Jack opened the white doors and prepared to see the horror inside.

When the crew entered, they saw what looked to be a surgical room. There were pales of animal blood. Otilia had to hold in her urge of puking. There were also body bags that weren't there when Clarke was exploring. The crew couldn't help but feel disgusted by the room.

"Oh dear, are those body bags?" Otilia asked.

"There sure look like it. Probably will be used as a ritual," Frank answered.

"We'll put an end to that soon," Jack replied.

"I sure hope so," Frank told Jack.

Looking around the room, the crew there were surgical tools around. These ranged from pliers, yankers, drills, and knives.

"I got a bad feeling Carlos is doing more than just rituals here. These poor souls might be test subjects in his sick experiments," Jack said.

"That or they might be food for his rats," Otilia replied.

The investigation only became grimmer as they saw more religious figures on a cabinet along with lit candles. Not to mention, the smell was rather unpleasant. There was another double door just ahead. When they tried to open it, they couldn't. Jack and Frank tried to pull on the edges, but the door wouldn't budge.

"Damn, it won't budge!" Jack shouted.

"I got a feeling this door doesn't open manually. There might be some secret button or pattern we have to figure out," Frank responded.

The crew looked around the room for any keys or panels to open the door. However, they found nothing of the sort. They saw that right side of the room was still not explored. The crew explored the rest of the room.

***

Clarke and Jessie woke up. They found themselves tied up on a surgical bed.

"What is this? Why are we tied up?" Jessie asked.

"Good question," Clarke answered.

Clarke and his daughter knew something was wrong when they woke up.

"All I know was that you fell to the floor and I tried to wake you up. Out of nowhere, somebody grabbed me and put me to sleep," Jessie said.

"I feel a hole in my neck. That might have been a sleeping dart. I suspect we're not the only ones here. There's something big going on here," Clarke replied.

Both of them struggled to escape, but the leather straps were tight. They knew something was wrong when they saw the surgical tools next to them. There were a lot of machines and test tubes around. That is when they realized they were in a laboratory.

"Is it me or are we nothing more than an experiment?" Jessie asked.

"It's not you, baby. I got the same feeling. We gotta get out of here!" Clarke said.

Clarke saw there was a sharp knife on the table to his left. His legs were freer than his hands. Clarke figured if he could reach the knife, he could cut the leather strap around him. With that in mind, he stretched his legs as much as possible. Clarke's leg was touching the table. All he had to do was pull the moveable table in his direction.

Pulling it proved difficult as he couldn't get a good grip on the table with his feet.

"Come on, papa," Jessie cheered her father.

"Come on, come on. Come a bit closer," Clarke said.

The table started moving on closer to him. Jessie became encouraged, figuring her father could get them out. As Clarke pulled the table, Jessie saw a couple of small tubes with rats inside. They appeared to be floating in a green-like liquid. She had a bad feeling that it was a virus that enhanced their ability.

To her left, she saw pictures of what appeared to be a humanoid rat. She put two and two together. Jessie realized that whoever was behind this was trying to breed humanoid rats. She just couldn't figure out why.

"How is it going, father?" Jessie asked.

"Just a little more..." Clark answered.

The table came even closer. Before Clarke made any more progress, a mysterious man entered the room. The man grabbed the table and pulled it back.

"Nice try, but nice enough. Now be a good test subject and stay still!" The mysterious man said.

"Who the hell are you?" Clarke asked.

"If you really need to know, my name is Carlos Rodriguez," Carlos said in a heavy Spanish accent.

Carlos had tan skin and looked like a man raised in Puerto Rico. He was wearing a lab coat with black jeans. He was bald and had a few tattoos on his arm that showed when he pulled up his sleeves. The tattoos were those of various deities in Santeria. The tattoos intimidated Clarke and Jessie. His face looked evil just by looking at it. He was a ruthless businessman who was willing to hurt anyone to get what he wanted, even his wife.

Carlos was a well-known person in Salinas for being a businessman. However, he was mostly a hated person in the community as he did next to nothing to help Salinas. The locals considered him nothing but a parasite, who took from the community and gave nothing back.

"You seem to have a beautiful mansion. So why do you have us tied up?" Jessie asked.

"My dear girl, I hate to say it, but you've been trespassing on my property. If you want to know what's going on, you two are my guinea pigs," Carlos answered.

"For what?" Jessie asked.

"I plan to clear Salinas out of all the heathens. For far too long, Salinas has been infested with non-believers. When Salinas is done, we'll move on to other parts of Puerto Rico until the island is under our control," Carlos answered.

"You must be one of those sick Santeria practitioners! I've heard of you bastards," Clarke retorted.

"I'm sorry that you misunderstand us. However, I have to say Santeria is perhaps the most misunderstood religion out there. We only wish to make Puerto Rico a better place," Carlos said.

"You mean a better place for yourselves and the rich!"

"No Clarke, for the Babalu! This is all for the almighty Babalu! I know it seems cruel to sacrifice humans and animals. However, I ensure you those heathens would have suffered in this world anyway. They are better off in the afterlife, where they can live peacefully with the other sinners. Meanwhile, we live in harmony here on earth. So it's a win/win!"

"Win/win, my ass! So you summoned killer rats to do the dirty work for you, heh?" Clarke asked.

"The rats were meant to be scavengers. They were only supposed to eat the dead bodies to cut down on burial costs. Sadly, they have a mind of their own. I admit my experiment wasn't perfect. However, I do feel bad just sacrificing people to please my god. So I decided those I deem worthy can be my humanoid rats to help clear out the bad people. Basically, that's the plan with you two. You aren't meant to die. Instead, you'll just be my slave."

"How considerate of you, but I would rather be dead than serve you!" Jessie retorted.

"Jessie!" Clarke was shocked by what he heard.

"It's true, papa. The last thing I want to be is a slave to this good-for-nothing piece of garbage!" Jessie retorted before being slapped by Carlos.

"You're a real man, slapping a young girl. I think my daughter is right about you!" Clarke told Carlos.

"Perhaps, but I don't care what you think of me. You guys are nothing but peasants. Besides, it's not like you have much of a choice in the matter. You're all tied up, quite literally as well," Carlos replied without remorse.

Clarke and Jessie knew they had no chance of convincing Carlos to have a change of heart. It was clear what Carlos' intentions were. The evil scientist pulled the table away from Clarke in case he had any ideas.

"I don't have time to waste. You just lay down there, my dear test subjects. I'll be back with the vaccine that will change your life forever. Don't resist! You will feel better joining me, trust me," Carlos told Clarke and Jessie.

"This isn't good! Help!" Jessie shouted, hoping someone would hear her.

"You're right. Our only hope is that our friends will find us. If not, we'll have to be rats for the rest of our lives. Not something I ever dreamed of being," Clarke replied.

Clarke and Jessie knew they were in the middle of a cult. Carlos had finally revealed himself as a sick bastard, who lacked any morals. Jack and the others had to hurry and find the lab.

***

Jack and the other crew members explored the right side of the room. They found more dead rat carcasses along with green blood. More importantly, they found a statue of Santa Barbara. There was an inscription below.

I, Santa Barbara, will only take the three most powerful African powers. Deliver them to me and the door to destiny will open.

In Santeria, Santa Barbara was considered the equivalent of the African deity of fire, Chango. Santeros used Santa Barbara to get around the idea of Santeria being a fringe religion. They did this by assimilating Catholic beliefs to mix with traditional West African religions. It was probably one of the most controversial religions in the world, with many calling it a cult over anything else.

"Oh great, a riddle," Jack said.

"The three most powerful African powers..." Otilia thought out loud.

"There are seven African powers in Santeria. We need to bring the top three here, but how?" Frank asked.

Otilia saw three square holes in front of the statue of Santa Barbara.

"I think we need to grab the small statues and place them in the holes," Otilia told the men.

"That makes sense. The problem is I don't know who are the top three. As I said, I'm not a total expert on the religion," Frank said.

"It'll be a process of elimination," Jack replied.

"Not so fast. If I know Carlos, this puzzle is probably booby-trapped. For all we know, we might only have one chance. If we get it wrong, we might get trapped," Frank said.

"I see some gas vents next to the statue," Otilia pointed out.

"Ha, they will probably spread a poisonous gas to intoxicate us," Frank responded.

The crew saw the statues of the seven African gods on the other side of the room. Everyone looked for a clue as to what the puzzle solution was. Nobody had any idea that Clarke and his daughter were about to be injected with a virus.

Everyone searched through the whole room. Nobody could find anything to help them find the solution. They didn't just want to guess, but time was of the essence. Jack slammed the bookcase next to him in frustration. After doing that, a binder fell.

He opened the binder and saw something that caught his eye.

The seven African powers

While all the African powers are paramount, there are three that are the most important to any practitioner of Santeria. They are Shango, Yemaya, and Oshun. These three are critical to pray to if you are to live a good lifestyle. Nonetheless, the seven-colored candle should suffice if you are doing any rituals. That is unless you are doing a prayer for a single power.

There was more after that, but Jack wasn't interested in the details. All he needed was the puzzle solution. He showed Frank and Otilia what he found. With the solution shown to them, the crew grabbed the statues of Shango, Yemaya, and Oshun.

Jack placed them in the order that was written in the note to be sure he didn't mess anything up. He had no idea if the order mattered. Otilia and Frank held their breath, hoping they were correct.

When the three statues were placed in their respective holes, the statues to Santa Barbara moved back. The crew checked the vent holes, but no gas was released. They all breathed a sigh of relief.

When the statue finished moving back, there was a red button. Frank pressed it. The previously locked door was now open.

"We did it," Otilia said.

"Yes we did, but I got a sick feeling whatever is behind that door will be grim," Frank replied.

"Hopefully, Clarke and Jessie are there, lest they've been taken out already..." Jack said somberly.

The crew walked through the door that opened. They were greeted with a blue hallway. It had a strong sterile smell as if they were in a hospital. It was also rather cold in the hallway.

"Wait a minute, this hallway has a weird smell," Frank said.

"Yep, it has that hospital smell. I bet there's a secret laboratory just ahead," Otilia replied.

"Wouldn't be surprised at this point. There's no use talking about it. Let's just keep moving," Jack told the crew.

As the crew moved through the hallway, they saw a door up ahead with a biohazard symbol. They were convinced there was experimenting taking place in the mansion.

The crew looked at each other as they prepared to uncover a disturbing plot. There was a panel next to the door. When Jack pressed the button, he expected there would be something blocking the door from opening. However, to his surprise, the door opened slowly.

Jack, Frank, and Otilia nervously anticipated what would be behind the door.

Chapter 23

Jack, Otilia, and Frank stared as the blast door rose. Jack and Otilia had their guns raised. Everyone had butterflies in their stomach. They knew that Carlos had to be in the laboratory. Nobody had any idea what Carlos was capable of.

The crew saw the laboratory filled with machines and test tubes. There was a corridor up ahead. That suggested the lab was larger than just one room. A horde of rats came out of the vent to scare the crew.

Jack and Otilia shot the rats as they came out of the vent. Frank would jump in the middle of any rats that got too close.

After defeating the horde, Jack and Otilia saw they had some ammo left. However, they didn't want to expend any more of it. There was no telling if they would need to kill Carlos or any giant rats. The corridor was filled with green blood, to Otilia's disgust. At this point, though, she was already used to seeing the blood. She wasn't as bothered as before.

When the crew walked through the corridor, they saw three doors. There was one ahead that read, main surgery room.

"I got a sneaky suspicion that Clarke and his daughter are beyond that door," Jack said.

The crew walked up to the door and saw it was locked with a key card.

"Of course... That leads me to believe there's something big beyond that door," Frank said.

"I'm almost scared to find out what is beyond that door," Otilia replied.

"Can't say I blame you, but we have to overcome that fear to save our friends," Jack told her.

"As long as you're here, Jack, I feel secure," Otilia said as she hugged Jack.

"I admit, Jack, you have kept us sane and protected. I owe you one," Frank said as he punched Jack in a friendly manner.

"It's not over yet, guys. Whatever is behind that door is probably disturbing as fuck," Jack told the crew.

They would need to find the keycard. To do that, they had to explore more of the laboratory. To start, they explored the left door. Jack and the crew walked through the automatic door.

Upon walking through the automatic door, the crew explored the large room. Inside there were many documents. Many of them proved useless for the crew. There was some equipment used for experiments, such as empty test tubes and syringes. Everyone looked in the drawers for a keycard, but none was found.

There was squeaking heard in the room. The crew looked around but didn't see any rats in the room. They assumed the rats had to be nearby. While there was no keycard, the crew found a box of .357 ammo and 9mm bullets. The extra ammo was welcomed by Jack and Otilia. Frank still had no weapon, but he didn't mind. He wasn't very good with a gun anyway.

Under the ammo was a document. Unlike the other ones in the room, this one caught the attention of the crew. They saw a picture of what looked to be a humanoid rat. There was a small passage below that they read.

Humanoid Rats

While sacrificing people is part of pleasing the great Babalu, I don't wish to kill everyone. Not every person needs to perish. Some people are worthy of life still. So the best way to ensure that happens is to make them my dear slaves. So why not make them into humanoid rats?

At first, I wanted to breed rats to help clear the human corpses. Besides, burying them would take too much effort. The rats would simply finish eating the dead bodies. However, the rats had an adverse reaction to my super vaccine. It seems they want to eat everything alive. Normally, I wouldn't mind, but there is a small danger that the rats could turn on me. I don't need that to happen.

Through research, I've found out that rats obey a master rat. I still don't know how to breed a master rat. I've found a loophole, though, humanoid rats. I can convert humans into rats. Once that's complete, the rats will obey the master rat. I'll have an army of slaves to help me clear the island of all the heathens.

I'm still trying to perfect the vaccine. It's been challenging to get the correct chemical balance. It needs to be perfect or the effects won't be what I desire. The life of a scientist can be so damn hard. At the same time, it's rather rewarding. Don't worry, great Babalu and dear brothers. I shall accomplish my mission. Even if it means getting a little help from science.

"Fucking bastard! He's gonna try to convert the population into rats! This guy is mentally lost at this point," Jack said.

"At this point, he might be better off dead," Frank replied.

"We have no time to waste!" Otilia shouted.

The crew left the room and went across the hall to the other door. When they reached the other room, they saw it was a security room. There was a television with cameras displaying. When they looked, they saw a camera showing a picture of two beds with two people lying on them. The cameras were black and white and of poor quality.

Despite the poor quality of the picture, Jack believed the two people were Clarke and Jessie. The room was ransacked in search of the keycard to the large door.

"Hurry up! I got a bad feeling Clarke and Jessie are about to turn into rats and I won't stand for that," Otilia said.

Despite their best effort, there was no keycard. There was a note on top of the desk. It said that the keycard was in experiment room #2. The room was just ahead. Jack and Otilia had their guns engaged. As the crew walked into the room, they saw a huge room with many capsules, machines, and experiment tables.

At one point, there had to be lots of scientists in the laboratory. Frank was dumbfounded that there was a secret laboratory in Salinas all this time. Then again, he knew that Carlos had money, so he could keep people shut.

"What is this place?" Jack asked.

"I never in a million years would've guessed there was an underground laboratory under this mansion. Carlos is clearly a mental case," Frank answered.

The crew walked around the room, hoping to find the keycard. Frank spotted the keycard in a holding chamber on the other side of the room. He typed in a few basic commands to open the chamber. After that, he grabbed the keycard.

As soon as he grabbed the keycard, Jack heard a loud screech. The crew looked to the other side and saw a giant rat break out of its cage.

"Holy shit! How do we defeat that bastard?" Frank asked.

"Just empty our bullets and hope for the best," Jack answered.

The giant rat was black and had large fangs, ready to eat the crew alive. The rat wasted no time going after the three of them. Everyone dived out of the way of the rodent. Jack and Otilia started to unload their bullets on the rat. Despite that, it didn't seem to have too much effect on the rat.

When Otilia wasn't paying attention, the rat whipped her with its tail. She struck a machine hard and fell to the floor.

"Otilia!" Jack shouted.

"Son of a bitch!" Frank said.

The rat started to go after Frank. He barely got out of the way as the rat slammed into a large experiment machine. The machine was destroyed instantly. Jack had to reload his magnum with the final six bullets he had. Frank was moving back in fear without a proper weapon. That was until Jack shot the rat.

"Find something explosive! I'll keep the rat distracted!" Jack shouted.

Jack did his best to distract the rat while Frank searched for something to kill the rat. The rat continued to go after Jack, who held off on shooting any more rounds. Otilia was still on the ground.

Frank went to the right side of the room, where he found some homemade grenades that could be used to blow the rat up. Jack was cornered as the rat attempted to bite him. He slipped away from the bite. The rat screeched.

"Come on, Frank! I can't hold this bastard back much longer," Jack shouted.

Jack shot the last two rounds of his magnum. Frank got the grenade and threw it at the rat. The impact of the explosion sent

Jack toward Frank, with both of them falling to the floor. As for the giant rat, its guts exploded and flew all over the room. The green blood was plastered all over the room. Some of it fell onto the crew.

Despite the gooey blood, the crew had survived the rat. Jack went to check on Otilia, who was still on the floor.

"Come on, Otilia! You gotta get up. The rat is dead," Jack spoke to her.

"I think you guys would make a good couple," Frank told Jack.

"Daww thanks, bro," Jack replied.

The two of them kept their eyes on Otilia. A minute later, Otilia opened her eyes to the relief of the men.

"Whew, you're still here," Jack said.

"What... happened?" Otilia asked weakly.

"We killed the big bastard. You were knocked out by that rat. However, you're up and we're happy to see you," Frank answered.

The two men helped Otilia back on her feet. Her head was killing her. She was still feeling a little dazed and fell to her knees.

"Oh man, she's still dazed. We can't let her go on," Frank said.

"I actually agree. Why not you stay with her while I go investigate," Jack told Frank.

"Me?" Frank asked.

"No worries, I trust you. I need you to make sure she's ok. I'll be fine. I'm sure if Carlos tries anything funny, I can handle it. I want to take her out, so take good care of her, ok?" Jack asked.

"I got you, bro. Just make sure Carlos doesn't harm our friends," Frank answered.

"Thanks and Carlos won't lay a hand on anyone,"

The men carried Otilia to the security room. There was a small bench, where they laid Otilia down.

"You can see me on the security camera. If you feel I'm in big trouble, come in and help me. However, please try to avoid leaving Otilia alone. It's time to save our friends," Jack told Frank.

Frank would keep an eye on Jack's potential future girlfriend. Jack was handed the keycard by Frank. The two hugged, knowing there was a chance they wouldn't see each other again.

Jack walked out of the security room. He walked to the blast door and inserted the red keycard into the reader. When the card was inserted, Jack saw the door open slowly.

He had no idea what to expect. Would he be in time to save Clarke and Jessie?

Chapter 24

Jack waited for the door to completely open. After the door was open, Jack walked inside. He saw a couple of surgical beds inside. He rushed toward them.

Clarke and Jessie were struggling to get out of the leather straps.

"Come on! We gotta get out of here or we'll be rats for the rest of our lives," Clarke told his daughter.

"I'm trying, papa. These straps are locked in too well," his daughter replied.

Jack could hear the voices of Clarke and Jessie coming from the other end of the large room.

Meanwhile, Carlos was in a separate room. He finished creating the green liquid virus that would turn Clarke and Jessie.

"Those two poor fools shall be my slaves forever. This is all for you, almighty Babalu. First, it will be Salinas. Next, it will be the rest of the island."

He grabbed the virus and inserted it into a couple of syringes.

Jack rushed toward the screaming, hoping to find his friends. A small horde of rats attempted to slow him down as he rushed toward the noise. He grabbed an iron pipe off the floor to fight off the aggressive rodents. One of the rats got onto him and bit his arm. He grabbed the rats and slammed the rodent on the ground.

More green-eyed rats attempted to attack him. Despite his arm being bitten, he fought off the rats with the pipe. The pain was stinging, but he fought through it.

Frank watched Jack over the security camera. He wanted to help Jack. However, Otilia was still knocked out. Frank knew better than to leave her on her own. He still had the wooden stick in case any rats entered.

As for Jack, he saw one last rat to his left. The rodent jumped toward him. He was well prepared and smacked the rat head-on with the iron pipe. The impact was enough to kill the rat instantly.

Green blood splattered on Jack. He could have cared less. In his mind, the green blood was already burned into his brain.

One of his shirt sleeves broke apart. He decided to rip the other sleeve of his shirt. Jack knew he would need a new shirt anyway. This wasn't the time to worry about how he looked. He wanted his hands on Carlos.

Back in the security room Frank was encouraged when he saw Jack still standing. He looked at Otilia, still sleeping.

"Otilia, you need to get up. We can't stay here, please," Frank told her.

He didn't get a reply. The good news was that she still had a pulse. Before he could get comfortable, he heard squeaking from the vent above him. The grate on the vent was busted open. A few rats entered the room.

With his stick, Frank fought off the rats. There wasn't much room in the room, so he had to stay put for the most part. Otilia started to wake up from her deep sleep. The first thing she noticed was that there were rats in the room.

Frank fought off most of the rats but was overwhelmed by the rest. Otilia quickly got up from the bench. She still had a few bullets for the pistol. Otilia shot the rats that were still alive to assist Frank. When Frank saw Otilia was helping him, he was encouraged to see she was up.

Between both of them, they kill the horde of rats that broke through. The two of them breathed a sigh of relief. However, the peace wouldn't last long. Otilia heard more squeaking coming from the vents.

"We can't stay here!" Frank shouted.

"Agreed, let's get out of here," Otilia replied.

The two of them escaped from the room and closed the door. They wanted to ensure that the rats couldn't follow them out. The two of them rushed into the main experiment room to catch up with Jack. As they closed the door, more rats took over the security room.

"Whew..." Otilia said.

"Let's catch up with Jack," Frank replied.

Back in the main experiment room, Jack saw he had no more bullets for the .357 magnum. He was a bit concerned if Carlos was armed. Jack had no idea that Otilia had recovered.

All bruised up, Jack continued to walk forward. He reached the source of the noise. Clarke and Jessie were seen all tied up on the bed.

"Clarke and Jessie! I'll get you out," Jack shouted.

"Am I glad to see you!" Clarke replied.

"Thank goodness you came. We're in a crazy house," Jessie said.

"Oh, I know. Carlos is one mental case. I better get you out of here before that maniac catches up to you. How did you end up here?" Jack asked.

"When we fell downstairs, we tried to find a way to get back upstairs to meet you. However, what we found was something far darker," Clarke answered.

"You mean the dead chickens and animal heads? Yeah, this nut is involved in some voodoo shit. I don't have time to explain right now. We gotta get you out of here," Jack replied as he tried to find something to cut the leather strap.

"Where are the others?" Jessie asked.

"They are in a security room. They'll catch up when I get you out of here," Jack answered.

Jack found a small knife that would cut the leather effectively. He started to cut the strap off Clarke.

"Try to hurry up before Carlos returns," Clarke told Jack.

"Don't worry. I got you. We'll be out of this hell hole..." Jack was cut off.

"That is if you get out of this 'hell hole'. I don't think you'll be escaping!" Carlos told Jack.

"Son of a bitch, so there goes the crazy bastard in real life. Your game is over. I'm ending this cult right now. You've performed your last sick ritual!" Jack retorted.

"I'm sorry to disappoint you, but I don't think you're in the position to threaten me," Carlos pulled out a dart gun.

Carlos shot a tranquilizer dart at Jack. It hit him on the arm. Jack started to feel tired as he fell to his knees.

"So close, yet so far. Too bad," Carlos taunted Jack.

"Damn you, Carlos. Damn, you and your screwed-up cult!" Jack retorted.

"No worries, you can join your friends. You'll all be slaves for the rest of your life," Carlos replied.

Jack did the best he could to stay awake. The tranquilizer was proving to be strong, however. Carlos saw his opening to inject his virus into the crew. Otilia and Frank rushed in and saw what was happening.

"Not so fast!" Otilia shouted.

She had her pistol aimed at Carlos.

"What you're gonna do, shoot me?" Carlos taunted Otilia.

"Don't push me! Let my friends go. I'm not afraid of you. You're nothing but a sick man believing in a cult. Karma will come back to bite you in the ass!" She answered.

"It's people such as yourself who give us a bad name," Frank told Carlos.

"No, it's the other way around. I will cleanse the island of all you heathens. The rats are just my dear assistants, is all. Besides, Salinas is just a causality of war, so to say," Carlos continued to taunt the crew.

Frank was upset as he took the gun from Otilia and prepared to shoot Carlos.

"You won't do anything. Just put the gun down, fool," Carlos said.

"What makes you think I won't blast your brains, you worthless piece of shit?" Frank asked.

"It's simple, people in Salinas are weak. They have no balls!" Carlos taunted the people of the town.

"Fuck you!" Frank shouted.

Frank pulled the trigger on the pistol, but it didn't shoot. He tried shooting again. Once again, the gun didn't fire. The gun was empty.

"Aww... your gun is empty? That's too bad. You had your chance to take me out. You failed! Now it's my turn," Carlos taunted Frank.

Before he shot his tranquilizer, Carlos saw a horde of rats behind him.

"I won't shoot you. I see a better way for you to foresee your doom. My dear rats will finish the job. Go ahead, young ones, clean out the heathens. This is all for you, babalu! Goodbye, my friends. I hope hell proves to be a wonderful place for all of you," Carlos said.

"Carlos, using rats to do your dirty work is just how I imagined things. You're pathetic. At least, be a man and do the task yourself," Frank retorted.

"I'm so sorry. Words don't hurt me. However, the bite of my mighty rats will sure will. It's time to enjoy your demise!" Carlos replied.

The rats moved closer to Frank and Otilia. When they got within striking distance, Carlos' face was shining with glee.

"Goodbye, suckers!" Carlos said.

After saying those words, the rats turned around in his direction.

"Wait a minute now. Rats, attack them. That is an order!" Carlos told the rodents.

"You forgot one thing, rats are still animals. They don't have to listen to you," Frank told Carlos.

"No, this can't be. I'm your master. You're supposed to obey me. Now go attack them!"

The rats ignored Carlos and moved in his direction. When he realized that the rats were after him, he panicked and started to run.

"No, get away from me!" Carlos shouted as the rats started chasing him.

With Carlos distracted, Frank got some water and splashed it on Jack's face to wake him up. Otilia grabbed the knife to cut the leather straps off Clarke and Jesse.

Carlos continued to run from the rats. He was getting a dose of his own medicine. The rats had him trapped in the corner of the room.

"No, Babalu! Why have you forsaken me? I did the best I could!" Carlos shouted.

"Your god has forsaken you because he's a phony god! Your cult is filled with lies and hatred. My father always taught me that hate will always lose. You are about to find that out the hard way. Where's the Babalu now? He's moved on to the next fool who's willing to give up his morals. I hope you enjoy your demise, it's well deserved!" Frank answered Carlos.

The rats ganged up on Carlos. When they got onto him, they had a ball tearing him limb from limb. Carlos screamed in pain but no one was going to help him. In fact, Frank had a smile on his face as he watched the rats get even with their 'master'. Frank felt that Carlos got exactly what he deserved for practicing Santeria.

It might have been only one person. However, Frank was satisfied that at least one practitioner was heading to his proper hell.

Carlos's flesh was torn off. The rats were enjoying their meal. It didn't seem they were in a rush to stop eating Carlos alive.

Meanwhile, Jack recovered from his tranquilized state.

"What happened?" Jack asked.

"That bastard tried to put you to sleep. However, he's getting a dose of his own medicine," Frank answered.

"Thank you for freeing us," Clarke said.

"Not much time to thank me, those rats will turn on us soon enough. We gotta get out of here," Otilia replied.

When Jack got up from the floor, he saw a key that was dropped by Carlos. It had the tag 'electrical room' on it. He quickly picked it up. The rats were devouring Carlos, a fate he clearly deserved.

"I got the key to the electrical room. We can cut the power to the gate and get out of here!" Jack shouted.

Everyone followed Jack as they escaped the lab. When the rats finished eating Carlos, they started going after the crew.

"Oh crap, they're after us!" Jessie shouted.

Everyone ran from the rats. They got to the hallway of the basement. Jack quickly unlocked the electrical room door. When they got inside, they saw the circuit breaker that powered the gate. Jack pulled on the breaker to cut the power off.

"Ok, I got the gate powered down. Let's get the fuck out of this crazy house!" Jack told everyone.

The rats continued to give chase as the crew rushed upstairs. They reached the main hallway and escaped through the front door. There was little time to waste as the rats continued to chase them.

Jack, Clarke, and Frank all headed to the gate to manually pull the gate open. It was a heavy gate. With the efforts of everyone, they pulled the gate open. Jessie and Otilia turned on both the SUV and truck. Everyone got into their respective vehicles.

The rats were out of the mansion, still chasing the crew. Jack and Clarke floored it as they drove out of the neighborhood. They turned to the right in a knee-jerk reaction. Jack and Clarke drove away enough to lose the rats.

"Whew, we finally got out of that hell hole. The sun should be coming up soon. That will make it easy for us to head to Camp Santiago. It's not over yet, guys," Clarke told everyone.

"It might not be over, but at least that crazy nut, Carlos, got what he deserved," Otilia replied.

The crew saw there were some emergency vehicles up ahead, to their relief. Help had finally arrived. Jack and Otilia held hands, figuring the worst of the adventure was over. While Otilia and Frank would probably have to find somewhere else to live, at least they still had a life to live.

The sun was starting to rise. The rats that chased the crew went back into the mansion to finish Carlos off.

One question remained. Was the rat infestation spreading further? That was something the crew would have to find out at a later time. For now, they just wanted a moment of tranquility where they could share their stories with others.

As they got closer, they saw police cruisers, but no people were around. The crew could only wonder why the cars were sitting there without an operator. They feared that the survivor horror adventure was far from over. At the very least, they still had their lives.

The End

Some cool sites to check out!

I hope you enjoyed this read as much as I enjoyed writing it. Anyway here are some cool groups you should check out on Facebook. Of course this is not the last book you'll see from me. I'll pop back out here and there.

Written Undead:
https://www.facebook.com/groups/350755889111261

Asylum of Fear:
https://www.facebook.com/groups/393167157937666

The Asylum Podcast Page:
https://www.facebook.com/groups/2997507817227314

Club Kaiju - LitRPG, fantasy, sci-fi, Harem, post-apoc,horror & YA: https://www.facebook.com/groups/484560235438701

Indie Horror Novels:
https://www.facebook.com/groups/257266748839272

Finally if you loved the book, please leave a review. Us indie authors depend on these reviews to make our dreams possible. So show the love and I'll be back soon with more.

Printed in Great Britain
by Amazon